P9-DNA-478

GONE TO
DRIFT

GONE TO DRIFT

Diana McCaulay

HARPER

An Imprint of HarperCollins Publishers

Library of Congress Control Number: 2017944339
ISBN 978-0-06-267296-4

Typography by David Curtis
18 19 20 21   CG/LSCH   10 9 8 7 6 5 4 3 2 1
❖

Originally published in the UK in 2016 by Papillote Press
First US Edition, 2018

For Fred
(aka my marine biology textbook)
and for the much abused Caribbean Sea

1

The boy sat beside the crumbling wall and stared out to sea. It was full dark and rain hissed on the water, but he was sheltered from the downpour where he sat. He saw a swirl of phosphorescence in the sea, gone so quickly he might have imagined it, might have merely wished for it because it was his grandfather who had told him about the tiny creatures that lived in the sea and at night shone blue in the wakes of boats and drew the deep ghostly shapes of fish. His grandfather said Kingston Harbour had once been full of them, that no night's fishing would have passed without seeing the shining mystery. "Where they go, Gramps?" the boy had asked.

"Sea too dirty for them."

"Why the sea get dirty?"

His grandfather had grunted. He was a man of the sea, not a man of words. Now Lloyd was sure he was lost at sea.

No one else was worried yet. Maas Conrad was only a day overdue from his trip to the Pedro Bank.

"Lloyd? But where the pickney is, eeh? Him is pure crosses. Only the good Lord know the trouble I seen." It was his mother's voice. Lloyd stood and turned to meet her. "You want get sick, pickney?" she said. "Out here inna the pourin rain a nighttime?" She stood under the brightly colored umbrella someone had left on the bus and she had taken. "Come. You grandfather be awright. You think the sea can kill him?"

Lloyd walked toward his mother and the shelter of the umbrella and together they walked through the dark streets of Kingston, the rainwater sweeping the streets, hiding the smell of human waste, taking the garbage of the city into the sea. Lloyd heard his grandfather's voice in his mind: *I come from a line of fishermen.*

Lloyd held the umbrella while his mother struggled with the front-door padlock of their small house near Bournemouth on the edge of Kingston Harbour. The nearest streetlight had blown many years before. His mother kissed her teeth. "Me tired to tell you wut'less father to buy one new lock," she said. Finally, the lock scraped open and they went inside. The air was full of water and the house was damp. "Go to bed, pickney. As God is my witness, you nah be a fisherman. As God is my witness."

He went into the narrow room at the back where he slept and untied the shower curtain tacked to the top of the door opening. There was no lightbulb or lantern in his room but light from the only other room in the house crept under the curtain, which smelled of plastic and mildew; smells of home to him. There was no window in his small space and he imagined it was like a cabin in a ship, below the waterline. He had never been on a big ship but he had seen them in Kingston Harbour making their slow way into and out of port—containerships, tankers, ships picking up gypsum from the gypsum wharf or flour from the flour mill, sitting in a cloud of dust as they loaded up. He thought of them as sea buildings, sea businesses.

He stripped off his wet clothes and hung them over the sagging line that held his school uniforms, pushing the uniforms to one side to make space for his undershirt and shorts. He dried himself with his rag and changed into the torn briefs he wore at night. He sat on his cot and felt hungry. Had he finished the bun from lunchtime? He thought so, but looked through his backpack just in case he had left a small piece. He found only the wrapper and he licked it for the crumbs, for the cinnamon and sugar smell.

"Lloydie?" his mother called as the wrapper crackled. "You hungry? Some fry sprat and bammy is here; come nuh?"

"Me awright," he answered, although saliva flooded his mouth at the thought of fried fish and bammy. His grandfather might be hungry, wherever he was, so Lloyd would be hungry too. He lay down and closed his eyes. He saw *Water Bird* alone at sea on a moonless night, lost, missing land by miles.

Why had his grandfather gone to the Pedro Bank? He was not a Pedro fisher. A man had to motor almost sixty nautical miles to find the Pedro Bank, sixty miles in an open boat, with no navigational equipment, no radio; just eyes and experience and stamina. The Pedro Bank was an underwater mountain southwest of Jamaica with three small cays—Top Cay, Middle Cay, and Bird Cay—and the fishing was still good. Although Gramps knew how to find the Pedro Bank, he never went there. He fished instead at Bowditch and the California banks and where the bottom of the sea fell off into the deep.

There were few fish inshore these days. Of course there were the fishers who cast their lines and nets close to the old sewage pipes emptying into Kingston Harbour where the garbage floated, and they did catch fish. But Lloyd's grandfather was not one of those men. He did not sell his fish to the women vendors who used burial fluids to make the fish look fresh. He would never use dynamite or chlorine to kill fish and make them float to the surface. No one had to tell Gramps when lobster season closed, or that Queen conch never lived where there were shattered conch shells on the floor of the sea, or that parrot fish should be left to graze the reef.

Maas Conrad was a deepwater fisherman, a line fisher. He did not use nets or pots, because, he explained, those methods were wasteful, catching everything above a certain size: trash fish, juveniles, eels, turtles.

Lloyd had first gone to sea with his grandfather before he was a year old, so his mother said, just for a spin around the Harbour, over the shoals of gray and green, into the flat calm water of the Port Royal mangroves. His mother said he had not cried. Later, when the boy had

learned an awkward doggy-paddle that he could keep up for many hours

in the water, he wondered about that first sea trip, which he did not

remember: Where had he sat in the boat? What would have happened

if the boat had hit a reef and sunk? He was sure his grandfather would

have carried him safely in his arms to land.

I am Conrad, Maas Conrad they call me, except for my grandson Lloydie, who calls me Gramps, and I come from a line of fishermen. When I was a boy, we lived in a fishing village called Great Bay, part of the Treasure Beach area of Jamaica's south coast. We were a family of six sons and we lived in one of the concrete nog houses set back from the beach, on a small hill. My father took us all to sea, one at a time, each in our turn. I was the youngest and, as I watched my brothers leave and go to sea, I longed to be with them.

They came back telling of things I wanted to see for myself, dolphins and sharks and leaping rays, turtles as big as canoes and the royal colors of marlins and jewfish that hid in underwater caves. They told of a kind of jellyfish that floated on the surface of the water like a plastic bag, a man of war, they called it, and they said it had stinging tentacles so long and so long-lived they could sting you days after the jellyfish had died. They listed the names of different types of sharks—nurse and tiger and mako and hammerhead and white tip. They talked of barracuda and dolphin fish and cutlass fish and wahoo and mackerel and how to take a wenchman off a hook, holding down the dorsal spines so they would not stick into your palm and get infected.

They learned to swim and use a mask and snorkel and a spear gun. They learned to draw a seine net and make a fish pot and where to go with a hook and line, up on the slabs of rock on the bluff. They knew about the phases of the moon and tides and when the sea breeze came up and when it died. They knew where and when the kingfish ran and when it was not safe to eat a barracuda. They learned to drive a boat and repair an engine, and one by one I saw their muscles grow, and their spines lengthen, and their eyes turn to slits suitable for staring at horizons. They became men on the sea, men in fishing canoes, men in bars with stories. They became big men in the community while I was still a boy.

2

Next morning, Lloyd woke early. It was a Saturday in August, just after the long Independence weekend, and the summer heat made it impossible to sleep late. His mother had left the house to meet the fishers as they came to land, to buy the best fish. Already? Lloyd thought. A new fisher already? She should wait. Suppose Gramps come back with his fish, and she done buy already? Had his mother already written off his grandfather?

He wondered where his father was. Vernon Saunders did not live with them, but he visited often and filled the two-room house with complaints. Lloyd did not understand how Gramps could have had a son like Vernon. Maas Conrad never complained. For him, words were used to get things done. Pass the bait bucket. Leaving at four sharp. Squall coming.

But his father talked a lot. The house was too hot; they must get a cheap fan from Princess Street. He had been fired again, but it had been a stupid job, not enough money. He had plans, ambitious plans, he could be somebody, but the big man was against him. His friend Selvin was fixing up a car for him, nothing fancy, but he could run taxi with it. And there was a money job coming up, a secret job.

Although when times were especially hard, Lloyd's father did go to sea with Selvin. Vernon was a sometime fisher, for he said fishing was for old-time people. The most frequent sentence he sent Lloyd's way was: Bring me a rum, bwoy. And his mother would always retort: You bring any rum inna the house? When you bring rum, then you get rum.

Lloyd did not look forward to his father's visits, but as he dressed that August morning, he wondered if he had heard anything about Maas Conrad or if the fishers at the Gray Pond fishing beach had news. Perhaps one of his father's friends who hung out at the beach might know something. Lloyd decided he would find his best friend, Dwight, and they would begin looking for Gramps. He was glad it was the summer holidays and he did not have to go to school.

The fish and bammy were still on the two-burner stove from last night, covered with an oily cloth. He ate with his fingers, standing, looking out of the front-room window. The rain was over and the morning shone. He could see a slice of Kingston Harbour—it was calm. He especially loved to be at sea on calm mornings, when *Water Bird* would skim across the water, stern low, bow high, and the speed was the best kind of drug. He preferred big waves to the usual chop of Kingston Harbour and calm seas best of all. He liked the days when not even the slightest of breezes ruffled the surface of the sea and he could stare down into the water and see what it held—sea grasses and coral and small schools of fish. He longed to be on a boat. He licked his fingers, loving the oil and the salt and the taste of fish. Should he wait for Dwight or go alone? His friend would not be up this early.

He finished dressing and left the house. His mother would be angry to find him gone when she returned; she would want his help with the Saturday selling. His mother did not sell her fish on the Harbour's fishing beaches or in the downtown markets. She took Maas Conrad's high-value catch uptown to an old fridge turned icebox on the side of the road near a Liguanea supermarket. She was Nicey-the-fish-lady, and the white people from Jacks Hill and the brownings from Mona trusted her fish. "You have lobster next week?" the women would ask from the windows of their huge cars. "I only buy fish from you, Nicey," they would say.

"Mebbe next week," his mother would reply. "But why you don't try this nice-nice silk snapper?" That was why his mother was called Nicey; her fish was always nice-nice. Her real name was Beryl. "Next week, Nicey," the uptown women would say as they pulled out into the stream of cars. Lloyd thought the uptown people were like sharks, certain of their status, unafraid of the multitudes of other creatures with whom they shared a home, barely noticing them. A shark could turn on a small fish at any time, and in the flick of a tail and the crunch of jaws it would all be over. He never made eye contact with the uptown people.

He walked toward Gray Pond, squinting in the rising sun over Long Mountain. In the distance, the stacks at the cement company were without the usual cloud of dust. If the plant was not working, it would be a good day for a swim at the nearby mineral baths. Maybe later he would do that—he would not be allowed into the proper baths, of course, not unless he could pay the entrance fee, but the springs found their way under Windward Road and came out at the edge of Kingston Harbour, and there boys often swam in a shallow canal edged with reeds. He liked the slightly metallic taste of the mineral springs, he liked the coldness on his limbs—it was a much better bath than the sponge bath in the outhouse at home, and he loved to let the slow force of the springs take him into the sea.

People said Kingston Harbour was polluted and he knew it was true; the sewage and garbage of the city ended up there, and the soot of the factories, and the oil and bilge of ships, but he was not afraid of the Harbour's waters. He made sure he did not swallow the water and always washed off in the fresh water of the springs.

"Mornin, Miss Lavern," Lloyd said to Dwight's mother. She was sweeping up breadfruit leaves in the yard. Lloyd looked up. The tree was bearing and the breadfruit would soon be ready for roasting.

"Mornin, Lloydie. You hear from Maas Conrad?" That was the way of it. His mother could pretend there was no need to worry yet, but the community of fishers and vendors and Harbour dwellers knew when someone was lost at sea.

"No, Miss. Nuttn yet. But is only two days."

"Is true. Maas Conrad be awright. You want Dwight? Him inside, still sleepin. That bwoy can't wake a mornin time."

"Me going talk to the fishers at Gray Pond beach. You can tell him for me?"

Miss Lavern nodded. "Maas Conrad have a cell phone, don't?"

"Ee-hee. But mebbe the battery dead or it fall inna the sea."

"True-true." Lloyd could see she did not believe Maas Conrad had let his phone battery die, or that he had lost his phone. It *could* have died, he thought. Surely it would be hard to charge a phone on the cays of the Pedro Bank, where the fishers stayed. And there *could* have been bad weather, the phone *could* have got wet and stopped working. Perhaps when he went to the beach he would see Gramps pulling *Water Bird* out of the water.

Lloyd had never been to the Pedro Cays. His grandfather was dead set against it and his mother had listened to the old man. The most daunting thing about the trip to the Pedro Cays was the possibility of missing them entirely in the dark, the five hours becoming six and then seven and then eight. Then, as the dawn turned the black sea gray and then navy blue, there would be no sign of the turquoise water of the Pedro Bank rising from the seafloor, no sign of three small cays in the middle of the Caribbean Sea. There would be the awful knowledge that the next stop was the coast of South America, that gas would soon run out and the boat would be at the mercy of the sea, spinning and wallowing like a coconut, taken south and west.

A man who missed the Cays would eat the raw and rotting fish in his bait bucket until it was done, he would vomit until all he had left was dry heaves and cramps, he would take tiny sips of the warm water in his plastic bottle, and he would pray for rain, for clouds, for anything to dim the sun, and he would stare at the water level in the bottle going down and down. It happened once or twice a year—Jamaican fishers would be found by foreign boats, starving and dehydrated, sometimes driven mad by exposure and hopelessness, by the sight of the endless sea and by the possibility of food fish under the hull of the boat, but too deep, too speedy to be caught.

Lloyd thought of Slowly from Gray Pond, a young man, not yet properly schooled in the ways of the sea, who had left alone on a reckless journey to Pedro years ago. He had missed the Cays and many days later had been picked up by a South American fishing boat, most likely on its way back from fishing illegally on the Pedro Bank, arrested by the authorities and jailed for almost a year. He came home speaking fluent Spanish. The fishers said he had lived because his boat passed through a mat of seaweed and he scooped it up in his bait bucket and there were tiny creatures in it. He ate the seaweed and the seabugs and this saved his life.

After Slowly came back to Jamaica, after he had been in the newspapers and on TV, after men in bars stopped asking him to speak Spanish, he became one of those thin men who haunted the fishing beaches of Kingston Harbour, skin blackened by sun and dirt, begging not for food or water or money or work, but for ganja, which would bring him some relief from his memories and his hunger. The fishers of Gray Pond said he still ate seaweed, when he could get it from the deep sea.

The women buying fish were leaving when Lloyd got to the Gray Pond beach. He stood where the road met the beach and cast his eyes east and west. He knew instantly there was no sign of *Water Bird*, which was painted bright yellow with a red bow cap. At the end of the beach under a divi-divi tree, older fishers mended their nets and pots. Lloyd walked over to them. "Mornin, Maas Rusty, Maas Benjy," he said. The men nodded in response, but did not look up from their work.

"You want some help?" Lloyd said to Maas Rusty.

"Is awright, yout', me soon done," said Maas Rusty. "You lookin for you granddaddy?"

"Just checkin, seein if him come back. You been out at Pedro?"

Maas Rusty shook his head. "Too many people out there in conch season. Me comin from Bowditch. But me did hear Maas Conrad was at Pedro."

"Yeh. Him call Tuesday, say him leavin Thursday mornin at first light. But him shoulda reach back now."

"What him was doin out there? Me never know Maas Conrad go Pedro yet."

Lloyd shrugged. He did not know why his grandfather had gone to Pedro.

"You check with the Coast Guard boat?" Maas Rusty said. "Them go out every Monday night. Everybody know Maas Conrad. Mebbe them know somethin. Mebbe him get sick and him restin out there."

"Me never see him sick yet."

"Any man can sick." Maas Rusty went back to mending the net and Lloyd felt there was more he wanted to say. A boat engine rattled behind them. Lloyd turned. Not *Water Bird*.

"You talk to you father?" said Maas Benjy.

"No. What him know? Him don't go sea more than so."

Maas Benjy shrugged. "Me hear them did have words, that's all."

"Words? What kinda words?"

Maas Rusty made a shushing sound and waved his hand at the other man. "Stop run up you mouth," he said. "After you no know nuttn. Check with the Coast Guard, Lloydie. That's you best bet. Go over Port Royal. Ask for Commander Peterson. Him awright. Him will talk to you. Mebbe him even take you out there."

"Lloydie!"

Lloyd turned and saw Dwight running across the sand. Gramps is back, he thought, Dwight has seen him, no, Dwight has seen his body, and he felt breathless and afraid, as if he had run to escape a beating. "You find him?" he said.

"Find who? You mother is at the house and she mad as hell. She say

17

she need you to help sell. You best get youself over there."

Lloyd turned to the old fishers. "Respect," he said. "You tell me if you hear anything?"

"Coast Guard," said Maas Rusty. "That's where you to ask." Lloyd turned and ran across the sand with Dwight to face his mother.

The sea was more real to us than the land, so now I find I cannot remember many details about our house, our school, or the look of the land. I know we slept three to a bed, by age, and as I was the youngest, I slept crossways at the foot of my brothers' iron bed. Often, I was kicked, but if I complained, they would push me onto the floor, onto my mother's rag mat, so I learned to make myself small and still. I can see the sash window, swollen from the salt air, stuck half open. I can see the kerosene lamp on an oval wooden table, the only other piece of furniture in our room. We took this lamp to bed at night and I can hear our mother's voice telling us to make sure the lamp was really out; we were to stare at it to make sure its last embers died because lamps had a way of flaring up again and burning down houses with children inside.

There was a big pond far behind our house, a salty lake that grew and shrank with rain and time. There was a time when it dried out completely and the sea breeze scraped the stinking dust from the bottom of the pond and coated our villages with it. That is why I remember the stuck sash window because while the dust whirled and settled we could not shut it out and our one thin sheet was full of grit. I did not mind the smell—to me it was a sea smell, caused by dying fish and a host of other animals. We did not know their names.

When the rain came, the pond filled and filled and found its way to the sea in small canals and winding trickles and the crocodiles—we called them alligators—came in and out. I do not remember ever being on the pond in a boat and now I wonder why.

Some boys tended their families' goats. Others had to weed the skellion fields. We all played fling-fling and roamed the area for whatever was in season—cashew, guinep, mango, pear. Our feet were tough from running on the few roads, made by women who broke the bigger rocks gathered by men. Mettle, we called those stony roads. Mostly the beaches were our roads. The fishing beaches were each of slightly different shades of brown and gray, with a black metallic tint that the waves pulled into swirling patterns in the sand. Great Bay had the widest beach and the sandiest bottom.

My mother's life was in the house and in the community. She was a big woman too, in her way, and I do not mean her physical size. No, I mean she was respected and known. She had a soaring singing voice and she sang in the church choir and she sang hymns as she scrubbed the floors and she sang as she chopped and cooked. She wore an apron every day, except on Sundays, when she wore a hat she kept in a box on top of the only cupboard in the house. On weekdays, she carried a basket and she tied a headscarf on her head. She bought our food at the Calabash Bay market, where the donkey men brought yam and sweet potato and tomato from the hill town of Mandeville and traded the produce of the land for sea fish caught by the men of the Treasure Beach fishing villages.

She hardly ever touched us. I did not ever wonder if I was happy.

3

Sales were good that Saturday, although the fish they had for sale was not Gramps's fish, not the best quality, and Lloyd was kept busy digging through the sharp chunks of ice to find the right type and size for the customers, wrapping the fish in newspaper, laying them in plastic bags. His mother had slapped him when she saw him, but it was a light blow, more for the benefit of Dwight's mother than meant to hurt him. Miss Beryl did not believe in giving harsh beatings to her son, although everyone in the community predicted badness as a result of this lack of discipline.

She punished him in other ways, and that morning he stood for hours at the side of the road, holding a large snapper in his hand. His arm hurt and so did his icy fingers, and the sun made him narrow his eyes to slits. His grandfather had shown him that trick—how to protect his eyes from the glare of the sea. As he stood at the side of the road in Liguanea, he thought of Gramps's gear—his hand lines, hooks, sinkers, anchor, knife, and gaff; his yellow rain jacket that smelled of plastic and salt and fish scales; his flashlight, cooler, bait holder. And his cell phone, now silent.

Traffic thinned out after lunchtime and there were only a few small yellowtail snapper left in the cooler. Miss Beryl sniffed at them. "Don't make sense take these home," she said. She never ate fish herself. It seemed strange to Lloyd that fish fed his mother but his mother never tasted them, did not know or care to know anything about the sea, or about the fish, where they were born and grew. She threw the leftover fish to the brown dogs that lived behind the supermarket.

That night, Lloyd's father visited for the first time since Maas Conrad had left for Pedro. He greeted the boy as he always did. "Wha'ppen, yout'?" he said. "You hear anything?" he said to Lloyd's mother.

She shook her head. "*You* hear anything?" she said. There was something hidden in her voice. She held out her hand and Lloyd's father gave her a bundle of folded notes. Lloyd saw it was much larger than usual and his mother stuffed it in her apron pocket without counting it. That was how they lived, how they ate—the money his father gave them sometimes and what they earned each week from the sale of Gramps's fish.

Late that night, Lloyd heard the muffled voices of his mother and father. He heard his grandfather's name more than once, and he wanted to get up and ask them what they knew but he was sure that would earn him another slap or worse. He was sure it was not worry that kept them talking about Gramps. He heard his own name, and he listened for anger in his mother's voice, or fear, because he was sure his mother loved the old man, but she did not seem to be angry or afraid. He thought he heard urgency in her voice. Black crab, she said. Perhaps catching crabs for sale was to be Vernon's next venture. He heard his own name and other words repeated. The dolphins. The dolphin people.

Lloyd knew there was a new thing in the Caribbean islands, places where tourists went to see dolphins kept in pools, where they paid a lot of money to touch them and swim with them. About a month ago, he had seen a dolphin stranded on the beach at Lime Cay, only fifteen minutes by boat from Kingston Harbour. The weekend uptown beachgoers had arrived to see the dolphin on the white sand beach washed by gentle waves, rocking this way and that.

Lloyd was at Lime Cay that day to help Miss Lavern with her bar and fried fish cook shop. He had walked over to the crowd around the beached dolphin and saw the uptowners on their cell phones. Soon the government officials arrived along with the dolphin people, who covered the animal with wet towels, and even held a tarpaulin for shade over the sleek animal, stuck on the beach. Lloyd wanted to kneel beside the dolphin, to look into its eyes, but a Syrian man with a big stomach and a loud voice kept everyone back.

Eventually, one of the big boats from the Yacht Club came and all the people helped to push the dolphin back into the water, scraping its skin on the sand, leaving faint trails of blood where the waves ran up the beach. There was a woman with the dolphin people, a slim black woman wearing a wet suit. Lloyd was impressed; he had never seen a black woman in a wet suit. She looked at home on the beach and in the sea and the men listened to her.

Lloyd recognized a few Port Royal fishers on the deck of the big boat. They lowered a kind of sling into the water, and the woman in the wet suit pushed the dolphin into the sling, her head lowered, her mouth moving as she whispered to the injured dolphin. Then the men strained and pulled and the sling came up, streaming water with a faint pink tinge. The dolphin twisted in the sling, trying to get away, bouncing against the hull of the big white boat, marking it with blood. The crowd on the beach clapped their hands and whistled when the dolphin disappeared over the weather rail of the boat and everyone returned to their beach towels and Red Stripe beers.

Later, Lloyd heard from fishers on Gray Pond beach that the dolphin had not been let go at sea, as he had imagined, but had been taken to one of the tourist places—attractions, they were called—somewhere in the north to be nursed back to health. The fishers laughed about this, the stupidity of it, the amount of money spent to rescue a single animal. They calculated the fuel cost to take the big boat to Lime Cay and then all the way around the coast to wherever the dolphin places were. Bare foolishness for a fish, the fishers said, even though they knew dolphins were different from fish. And after that, Lloyd heard that foreign men speaking Spanish came to Jamaican fishing beaches asking fishers to catch dolphins for them.

It was not steady work. Months or even a year would go by before the foreign dolphin traders would come to the fishing beaches. It was never the serious fishers who considered looking for dolphins for the traders, but Lloyd heard the talk. A young female them want, the men would say. A pretty one with a pink stomach. No mark on the skin. There were various stories about the traders—that they were friends of Slowly's from prison and he explained things to them in Spanish. Others said they were from countries on the other side of the world.

Listening to his mother's and father's voices, Lloyd wondered if somehow his grandfather had become involved with the dolphin traders. No way, he thought. Gramps loved dolphins. But perhaps he had seen something he should not have seen.

Lloyd stared into the darkness of his small room and made plans to find his grandfather. The Coast Guard. Pedro Cays. Maybe finding the woman in the wet suit. He thought about Maas Rusty and Maas Benjy talking about the words between his father and grandfather. Maybe his father was the place to start. Black crab, his mother said again from the next room. Listen to me, nuh?

I am thinking about the boats of my life, starting with the split surfboard my brother Luke and I found washed up in Great Bay one morning. We played with it in the shallows, daring each other to push it into deeper water. We were very young. And then we found a canoe made from one entire cotton tree, the tree felled, the inside scooped out, as long as the legs of the long-dead fisher who made it. We found it in a clump of macca bushes. We rocked it to get it loose, but it was too heavy for us. The seven Saunders men got it to the beach on one of the carts the fishers used to move their engines around, and it became our canoe. We scrubbed her sides with sand and we found an almost finished can of paint on a rubbish heap and we named our boat in crooked but proud letters—Birdie. I have always liked bird names for boats.

Birdie had no modern features, no engine, of course, but also no oarlocks, no cleats for tying a rope, no thwarts to sit on, nowhere to store gear so it would keep dry. You could see the marks of the tools that had been used to make her, although where we sat in the bottom was worn smooth by contact with human bodies. The hull was a half circle so there was no keel. If a man sat in her, she settled low in the water and had almost no freeboard, but Birdie never leaked—she was the most watertight boat of my life. She was a sturdy craft—once a wave carried us into the reef and it was the reef that suffered. She was most suited for a river, we thought, not for the risks of the sea, although we knew the Arawak Indians, who were Jamaica's first peoples, made such boats and went to sea in them. Birdie was our playground and playroom, not that we knew such things existed then, and there my boyhood and my youth was spent, in half of a felled cotton tree, a tree that lived on, a tree that went to sea.

Then there were my father's fishing canoes, two of them. He went to sea in one—Survival—and my oldest brother, Ben, in the other—Silver. My father had wanted to name his second boat after my mother, Sylvia, but the painter man had misheard him or perhaps could not spell and my father's second canoe, bought when I was about seven, became

Silver. *In time, I came to see it was a good name, a perfect name—so much about fishing had the color of silver.*

Before our father took us to sea, we merely played with the sea. Going to sea with our father was different—it was the first step to becoming a fisher. And Luke went to sea without me. While I waited for his return, I told myself stories about Birdie, *that she had been made and used by a young Arawak prince. Our school books had pictures of these Arawaks, naked to the waist with strange, sloping foreheads; peaceful people, it was written, who were expert seamen. I liked to think I had Arawak blood in me. I came—we all came—from a line of fishermen.*

A childhood memory now comes to me—I am searching for sea snails to use as bait, combing the rocks, pulling them from where they fastened themselves by tiny suckers. I would hold them up and they would send out their tiny bodies with two black antennas at the tip, like eyelashes. They would try to hold on to my fingers with their suckers. The sea snails all had black flecks on their shells but were shaded differently—green and pink and gray. Some were rounded, others triangular.

I remember the day I found a rock pool, a small thing, the size of a plate, but it seemed to me it contained the whole of the sea, the warm, constantly replenished water, the barely visible feathery plants and the sea snails, no two the same size, no two ever alike. A whole world in a small pool. I searched for two identical sea snails for my entire boyhood. Yet, I cracked them open with a rock to get at the meat inside their shells for bait.

I am on a rock in the Caribbean Sea. There are sea snails all around me now and I realize they are a source of food. They can neither fly away nor scuttle deep into a crevice in the rock where I now lie. These tiny morsels, full of bits of shattered shell, these will keep me from starving.

4

Lloyd waited outside the Tun-Up rum shop. All his mother's fish had sold the day before, and when she had counted out the money, she said there was no need for selling the next day. If Saturday sales were not good, his mother would miss church on Sundays and go again to her place at the side of the road in Liguanea. On this Sunday morning, his mother shook him from sleep, insisted he wash and dress in his church clothes, and they walked together to the Church of the Living God in Bournemouth. Lloyd hated church. He hated getting dressed up, he disliked the sweaty women who fussed over him and the voice of Pastor Errol, always talking about sin and fire and brimstone. He sat on the hard pew and wished to be at sea. He knew that by the time the service was finished, it would be too late to offer to crew for any fishermen. He bowed his head and let the singing and the shouting wash over him.

He would look for his father later that day at his favorite rum shop.

The rum shop was crowded and loud. Lloyd went around the back into a narrow lane with piles of garbage. He sat on a stone. He listened for his father's voice, but it was hard to hear any individual voice, hard to understand what the men were saying, as they shouted and cursed and slapped down dominoes. A herd of goats came around the corner and started to eat the garbage, pulling the piles apart. How should he approach his father? And when? There would be no point if he got too drunk.

Lloyd stood and peered through a dusty window into the dark inside of the bar. He saw the wide and solid back of Miss Lilah, the woman who owned the bar, and he saw the domino players, who sat outside on the sidewalk. The other men were shadows. He would have to go inside. He sighed. He was sure his father would not like his questions.

He hesitated, thinking of his grandfather's way of dealing with trouble. He remembered the time a sudden rain squall had blown over on the way home from Portland Bight, and how Gramps had turned the bow of the boat straight into the waves, away from home, the rain stinging their faces. They could not see anything except the rain and did not know what was ahead. His grandfather had held his course. He was a man who did what had to be done, the difficult thing, the right thing. When the squall was past, he turned the boat around and motored for home, the squall then ahead of them, smoothing out the sea. Lloyd walked around the side of the bar and went inside.

He saw his father right away, leaning on the bar, off to the left, a quart bottle of white rum in his hand. Lloyd tried to see how much rum was left, but it was too dark. As he watched, his father put the bottle to his mouth and Lloyd stepped forward—no point in waiting, his father would only drink more. He walked up to Vernon Saunders and touched his arm. His father shifted to one side, not looking to see who stood so close to him. "Pa?" Lloyd said. His father drank from the bottle again. The men shouted and laughed. "PA!" Lloyd said, more urgently. His father's head came around and Lloyd looked into his eyes. They were red.

"Lloyd? What you doin here? You want you mother kill you?"

"Come outside," Lloyd shouted over the noise.

"What?"

"Outside! Come outside!" Lloyd did not like to touch his father, but he tugged at his arm and pointed to the door. His father yelled, "Soon come!" to Miss Lilah and she nodded. Outside, the heat of the day was at its height. Vernon stood with his back to the sun and his face was in shadow. Lloyd squinted up at him, trying to read his expression. "What you want, bwoy?" his father said.

"You know Gramps don't come home Thursday. Him go to Pedro from Sunday and him don't come back."

"So?" Vernon took another long drink from the bottle of rum. "Him must just decide to stay. Fishin must be good. What you botherin me for?"

"Him not answerin his phone. You see him before him go?"

"Who you think you is, bwoy? To come here put question to me like you is police. You lick you head?" His father grabbed his arm and twisted it and Lloyd smelled Vernon's familiar smell of rum and sweat and ganja and dirty clothes. "Gwaan 'bout you business! Facety and outta order pickney." Vernon dropped Lloyd's arm and pushed him away. "Gwaan home, bwoy. This a big man place." He flung his arm at him in a go-away gesture.

Lloyd stood his ground. He took a step back but he did not leave.

"Me just want know if you did see him before him leave for Pedro. That's all."

"Me never see him. That crazy old man . . ."

"Maas Benjy say you and him did have words."

"Maas Benjy say *what*?" Vernon stepped forward and his hands closed on Lloyd's throat. "What you tellin me, bwoy?"

"Him say . . ." Lloyd fought for breath. He tried to pull his father's hands away, but he did not have the strength. He thought about drowning, sinking under the surface of the sea, a weight around his ankles, staring up to the light at the surface.

"Leave the bwoy alone, Vernon. What do you?" It was Miss Lilah. "You want get arrest for child abuse?"

"Don't chat rubbish inna me ears, woman," Vernon said, but he dropped his hands. "Don't him is my son? Is for *me* to decide how to deal with him." He slapped his chest.

"Gwaan home, Lloydie," Miss Lilah said, pushing herself between father and son.

"You mother awright?" Without waiting for an answer, she said to Vernon, "Modern time now. Can't just rough up a pickney inna the street like that. Go back inside." Vernon kissed his teeth and turned away.

"You hear anything 'bout Maas Conrad?" Lloyd said to Miss Lilah.

"No, youngster. Me hear say him don't come back. But mebbe him stop somewhere. Don't worry you head yet." Miss Lilah touched his shoulder and Lloyd wanted her help, her strong arms around him. He tried to smile and he knew his eyes shone with the tears he had been fighting since he woke.

"You a good lady, Miss Lilah," he said. "You will tell me if you hear anything?"

"Ee-hee, Lloydie. Gwaan now. You granddaddy be awright."

Unable to sleep that night, Lloyd left his mother's house and went again to the wall at the eastern end of Gray Pond beach. His mother never heard the scraping of the inside bolt if she was already asleep. He had to leave the front door unlocked, for to click the padlock shut would trap her inside. He made his way to the hollowed out place he had fashioned in the stones and lined with an old feed sack. He leaned against a wooden light post, the power lines now ran along the new concrete ones on the Windward Road, and he stared out to sea, looking for his grandfather. There was no moon. He settled into his post and the waves of the starlit night soothed him. He thought of the questions he used to ask when he was much younger.

"Why you go sea alone, Gramps?"

"Why you leave out so early?"

"Why some fish bite only certain time of year?"

"How you know what bait to use?"

"Why sometime you drop a line and sometime you trawl?"

"How you know where to go?"

"Why you don't wear a life jacket?"

I come from a line of fishermen was all his grandfather ever replied. And Lloyd would see that line of fishermen slanting into the sea; a line that could both feed you and cut you.

He thought of weekend trips with Gramps. He would leave for his anchorage at four in the morning, long before the garbage men started their work in the city and before the dancehalls turned down their music, in the coolest part of the night. He sat on the stern thwart of *Water Bird*, his hand on the engine, and Lloyd stood in the bow, holding the anchor rope to steady himself, staring ahead, taking the waves with flexed knees. They went together across the sea and they anchored and fished together. When the sun came up, and the ice cooler was full, and the fish had stopped biting, if the weather was calm, they went to one of the Portland Bight cays.

Tern Cay was Lloyd's favorite, off Needles Point, encircled by a reef that not many fishers could find their way through, the white sand coarse, the sandflies few. Under a single straggly mangrove tree, Gramps would roast an unscaled red snapper on a square of zinc, the snapper's skin crusted with salt, the fire small and hot, until the skin of the fish flaked off, leaving the pure white flesh for grandfather and grandson to eat in a thin sauce of seawater and onion and lime and Scotch bonnet pepper. Maas Conrad ate with his fingers and his favorite knife, which he cleaned by sticking into the sand where the waves broke.

Afterward, they rested in the small shade and Gramps told the boy dolphin stories. "Aah, me son, them animal smart so 'til. Them hunt together and them live together and them will even keep a man company a night-time. Sometime you hear them before you see them, you hear when them come up to breathe air like we. Them swim far and them dive deep. One time, over by Wreck Reef, when a big wave carry me over the reef, is a dolphin show me the way out."

Lloyd believed these stories less as he grew older, but he often saw the dolphins that came to the entrance of Kingston Harbour, and he loved their sleek bodies and the way they swam beside boats big and small, like police outriders for high-up people. In the old days, his grandfather said, no fisherman would deliberately harm a dolphin for it was well known that such an action would bring big trouble on a man's family.

The lapping of the waves pulled him into a restless, upright sleep and he dreamed of his mother's flat voice, stating what she knew for sure—as God is my witness, you nah be a fisherman.

My father was a black man and my mother was St. Elizabeth red with gray-green eyes. We Saunders boys were all different shades of brown. My father, though, was truly black; his skin reminded me of the Kiwi shoe polish we had to use on our school shoes. He came from Little Bay on the north coast, near to Negril, where the beaches were made of pure white sand. Luke was the lightest skinned of us all, with the greenest eyes. The market women called him "puss eye."

I was closest to Luke. We were the small boys, only ten months apart in age. There was a four-year gap between Luke and Colin, the next oldest son. That four-year gap was wide; Colin, Lewis, Robert, and Ben were the big boys. They called us tiki-tiki, after tiny fish. We were four to two; not three to three in our family. My big brothers were always men to me and I yearned to catch up with them. They were better at everything—catching lizards with nooses made from coconut trees, stoning mangoes, shooting birds with slingshots made from inner-tube rubber; better at football, better at cricket, better runners, better swimmers. They laughed at our efforts to keep up with them, but everyone knew not to bother the younger Saunders boys because the big ones would come to their rescue. The other members of my family swim in and out of memory, but Luke is always there, the witness of my life, and I, the witness of his. We grew up together; brothers, kin, friends. Sometimes we dreamed the same dreams.

When it came time for Luke to go to sea in his turn, I begged my father to take me as well. Ten months meant nothing, we were really the same age, I argued. My father was not swayed and although he threatened to beat me if I followed, I crept out behind them in the night and settled in the shadow of another old canoe, so long discarded on the beach that vines grew through its holes. I heard the murmur of my father's voice as he instructed Luke. The almost full moon was hidden by cloud and my father was invisible. What age were we?

I am not sure, maybe eight or nine.

We knew the sea, of course. It was the boundary of our world: the sea gave us smells and winds and weather and it was the subject of nearly all our conversation. The sea gave and it took. It was our food and our livelihood and our recreation, but it could kill men as well. My father often talked of the boat **Snowboy**, which went to sea with forty-odd men, twelve of them from our fishing beaches of Great Bay and Calabash Bay and Billy's Bay and Frenchman's. **Snowboy** foundered on the way from Kingston to the Pedro Bank in the deep sea. The newspapers said **Snowboy** had been overloaded. A search was mounted, but not a single man was ever found and the fishing villages mourned for half a year. The sea was vast and yet intimate, dangerous and yet holding us to her bosom, calm and also racked with furies. The sea was all.

It is that same sea that has brought me to this rock on the Pedro Bank, carved by the waves of centuries into jagged crests of gray and black. There is no tinge of green but there is life here: seabirds, crabs, snails, whelks. There are signs that fishers visit; human waste, a shelter made of a tattered tarpaulin, a plastic bottle tied to a rock full of warm, fresh water. I tried to catch one of the birds but they are much too wily. I catch a small ghost crab and crack it open. I close my eyes to eat the half liquid flesh and it slides down my throat. Perhaps the fishers will be back today and I will return to land with them.

5

Lloyd waited for the airport bus on Windward Road. It would take him to Port Royal where he would try to speak to someone at the Coast Guard base. He had waited until his mother left the house to buy the day's fish and then he washed and dressed in his church clothes from the day before. The only food on the stove was an end of hard dough bread. He made himself a cup of mint tea with three spoons of brown sugar. He sat on the front step and ate the bread. He would be in trouble when his mother found him gone.

He did not feel tired, despite his night-time wait on the old wall. Staring out to sea was as restful to him as sleep. He knew he had slept for a while, leaning against the light post. Gramps had told him that a man must be able to catch sleep where he can. Lloyd had seen his grandfather sleep in the inch of dirty water that always sloshed around

41

in *Water Bird*, no matter how much they baled.

He had never been to the Port Royal Coast Guard base. He knew their boats, *Cornwall*, *Middlesex*, and *Surrey*, named for Jamaica's counties. He thought they looked like battleships in a war movie, with their gray bulk and mysterious tangle of gear. They were anchored in the lee of the Palisadoes strip and any fisher leaving Kingston Harbour motored past them.

The gate to the base was right opposite Fort Charles, where an old-time English admiral had walked the walls in the famous town of Port Royal, right at the end of the Palisadoes strip. Lloyd often went to the fishing beach in Port Royal to crew for other fishers or to leave with Dwight and Miss Lavern for Lime Cay, but he had never tried to go inside the chain-link fence to the Coast Guard station.

The bus came and he boarded, paying the driver. It was almost empty and he sat by a window at the back. He needed a plan to get through the gate at the Coast Guard station to see Commander Peterson, the man Maas Rusty had told him about. He gazed out at Kingston Harbour, looking for the bright colors of *Water Bird*. Gramps could come home anytime, he thought. One minute the sea could be empty, and the next minute it could deliver his grandfather safely to land, as the sea had done over and over and over. He tried to convince himself that a man could not just disappear, not without trace, but he knew it was not true. A man, especially a fisherman, could disappear easily because the sea held many dangers.

He tried to imagine dying, but he could not. He could imagine violent acts and violent events, done to him, to his mother, to his grandfather, to strangers; he could hear the sound of gunshots, feel the pain of bones breaking, the fight for breath of drowning, but always his imagination stopped before the final end. In his mind, his father was always the one who held stick, gun, and rope.

Then he tried to imagine a world without his grandfather. A few days, even a week without him was normal—Maas Conrad lived alone at Springfield—but he ate with Lloyd and his mother at least twice a week, on nights when Vernon was not there. Gramps and Vernon did not get on. Lloyd wished he knew what had caused them to circle each other like wary dogs.

Lloyd knew bad things happened, but not every fear was realized. Perhaps if he told himself his grandfather was dead, then the opposite would be the truth. No one could tell the future and the worst things were always unexpected, and always lay wait in ambush. On the other hand, if a boy was sure his grandfather was dead, he would not look for him; he would not be on this bus on a Monday morning with workers going to their jobs at the airport. He could not fool the rules of the universe, of fate, of God. He should have paid more attention in church, perhaps he should have asked Pastor Errol to pray for Gramps. He could not make sense of his grandfather's absence. Was it too early to worry, or too late?

Too much thinking. It was time to act. He needed a plan to get through the Coast Guard gate. He wished he were a man in a suit in a white SUV, not a boy in too small, too warm church clothes in a JUTC bus.

The bus stopped near Harbour View and more people boarded. "After work, me going to Gloria's to eat a fish," a man said to one of the women.

"Huh. You lucky. Me on double shift today."

Gloria's, Lloyd thought. Maybe if he waited there long enough he would see Commander Peterson. The man had to eat. Maybe the commander would come out from behind the Coast Guard gate in his uniform and he would sit at a table at Gloria's and order lunch and perhaps that would be Lloyd's chance to tell him about Maas Conrad.

It is hard to sleep on this rock; it cuts into my back and the surf booms all night, but last night I slept enough to dream of my mother. I dreamed she was asking the men of Gray Pond beach to look for me but they refused. As the sky lightens, I remember her songs. I can taste her food. I can see her wearing a white dress and her church hat at our school prize-giving events, wiping her face in the heat. What I remember most about her is a feeling, a feeling of safety and plenty and homecoming. These were her gifts.

Growing up, I occupied a world of men, of men who went to sea, and we all pulled away from the world of women. I often wondered what it would have been like to have a sister. There were girls at the Sandy Bank primary school, but they were a territory we Saunders boys did not explore. We laughed at their skipping games, their ring games, their games of jacks, the songs they chanted in their high voices. We threw lizards at them and watched them shriek and run away. Now, I wonder if my mother was lonely in our male territory. She died young, before I left Great Bay. I was a young man just turned twenty, I do not know her age. Sickle cell, the doctor told us. Now, I wish I could speak to my mother, man to woman. I wish there was another chance to know her.

No fishers came to the rock today.

6

Lloyd saw it was too early for the lunch trade when he arrived at Gloria's. A young woman in a torn apron dreamily cleaned tables and the door to the kitchen was almost closed. The tables at Gloria's occupied the sidewalk and one of them straddled a trickle of wastewater in the gutter; it was made to sit level with folded up newspaper under two of the legs.

Lloyd looked around for a place to wait, and saw a bench outside a building across the street, but a man lay full length on it, his mouth open, his limbs trailing on the ground. He thought about various places in Port Royal where he could wait—Fort Charles, but there was bound to be an entrance fee there, the Port Royal Marine Laboratory, behind a gate with a security guard, and there was no chance a boy in church clothes could just walk into the Morgan's Harbour Hotel.

He walked to the familiar fishing beach and onto the rickety wooden dock jutting out into the Harbour. Here the smell of sewage was strong and there were few boats on the beach. Lloyd sat on the wood, bleached soft and smooth by years, and stared out at the oily calm of the Harbour. Anytime, he thought. The waves shushed and swirled around the dock. A stingray jumped out of the water right in front of him and Lloyd remembered one of Gramps's stories about the time a fisher had idly shot a stingray and thrown it into his boat. The dying ray had sent its barb through the wooden oarlock. "Respect," Gramps had said. "Him lucky it never catch him. And the ray was small."

Lloyd relaxed against one of the wooden pilings and squinted at the Harbour. Boats of all sizes went by—the small ones like buzzing insects, the large ones bulky and slow. He turned to watch the entrance to the Harbour and just rounding the point, he saw a figure standing on a surfboard. He couldn't tell the sex of the person—he or she held a long paddle, and, balancing on the swaying surface of the water, the figure dipped the paddle into the water on one side of the surfboard and then the other. Lloyd wondered if the wake of a boat would make the person fall over. It seemed a very inefficient method of transport, but he thought he would like to try it.

He watched the figure and realized it was moving faster than he had first thought. The paddle went up and down in a smooth, steady rhythm. He saw it was a woman in a wet suit and he wondered if it was the dolphin woman at Lime Cay, the woman who might know about the capture of dolphins. He had seen surfers out at Bull Bay riding the waves, but had never seen anyone standing upright on a surfboard with a paddle. A canoe zipped by the woman and with two strong strokes of the paddle, she turned the surfboard to face directly into the curving wake. Lloyd saw her bend her knees slightly and take the bounce of the surfboard with the paddle held across her chest.

He wondered where she was going—the hotel, he thought. He watched her come closer to the dock and when she was at the nearest point, he stood up and shouted across the water, "Hi! Miss!" He waved his arms and she turned to look at him, almost losing her balance. She stopped paddling and the surfboard continued to glide in the direction she was headed.

"Miss!" he called again. He wondered if he should swim out to her, but his doggy-paddle was slow and this part of the Harbour was dirty. He waited to see what she would do.

And she dipped the paddle and turned her board and in a few strokes was standing in front of him on the surface of the sea. He saw it *was* the dolphin woman. She was wearing a short wet suit, leaving her arms and legs bare. Her toenails were painted, but not her fingernails. Her hair was very short, almost shaved clean. Her eyes were the color of beer. "You call to me, yout'?" she said. Despite her black skin, he had thought her a foreigner because he didn't think a young Jamaican woman would be a dolphin expert. He was surprised to hear her speak with a Jamaican accent.

"You the woman what save that dolphin outta Lime Cay," he said.

"Last month," she agreed.

"What happen to it?"

"Died in the pick-up. Dolphins can't cope with gravity. You like dolphins?"

"Ee-hee. Where the dolphin was going in the pick-up?" Lloyd had not understood what she said about gravity.

"Don't know. Some other island, probably, but could be sold anywhere. Russia, even."

This seemed unbelievable to Lloyd but he wanted to keep the woman talking. "My granddaddy, he *love* dolphins," he said.

The woman smiled and rested her paddle on one end in front of her. She stood as if she were a sentry at a fort and the sea was solid ground. "Your granddaddy a fisher?"

He nodded. "A line fisher." He thought that was an important detail.

"Anyway . . ." she said, and he knew she was preparing to leave.

"Me never seen anybody stand on a surfboard like that. It hard?"

"Easy in calm sea. Takes awhile to get used to if it's rough. I like it because you can see far enough ahead. And it's slow. Relaxing." She laughed. "Sometimes the Harbour dolphins—you know them, right?—come up beside me and then I have to sit down. They'll make me fall over for sure."

"What's your name, Miss?"

"Jules."

"Miss Julie?"

"No. Jules. My father liked Jules Verne, you know, the book *Twenty Thousand Leagues Under the Sea*?"

Lloyd shook his head. He had no idea what she was talking about, but he was glad she had not left him.

"What's *your* name then? You live in Port Royal?" she asked.

"Lloyd. No, over by Bournemouth. Near Gray Pond beach. Looking for my granddaddy. He don't come back from Pedro three— no, four—days now."

The woman, Jules, inclined her head, as if asking a question. She made a short stroke with the paddle and the surfboard bumped against the dock. He saw it was tied to one of her ankles. She put the paddle on the dock, and then her palms, and without pushing off with her feet, she eased herself to sit on the dock beside him. They both looked out across Kingston Harbour. She gave a little sigh. "You live with your granddaddy?"

"No, my mumma. She sell fish in Liguanea. Gramps, he *never* go to Pedro, but he go this time and him don't come back."

"What, he don't have a cell phone?"

"Yes, him have one, but him not answerin it. Me come over here to see if the Coast Guard go look for him."

Jules turned to face him then. "And you couldn't get through the gate, right?"

He was ashamed to say he had not tried, so he just shook his head.

"You know the hotel? Morgan's Harbour?" she said. "Wait for me there. In the parking lot, under the almond tree. I'll take you over to the Coast Guard." She eased herself off the dock onto the surfboard, finding her balance right away. He watched her heading away from him, the surfboard trailing a faint wake. She did not look back to see if he would do what she had told him.

My four older brothers became Pedro fishers. I am trying to pin down the year in my mind. I suppose it was sometime in the fifties. Men were just beginning to go to the Pedro Bank from our villages. Before, fishers had to go on a bus to a place called Complex in Kingston, where they went to Pedro on big boats, like Snowboy, the one that disappeared. But engines were improving and fishers started to make the journey themselves, leaving late at night. The journey was long and there were the twin dangers of bad weather and poor navigation that could get a man lost at sea. No fisher went to Pedro alone in those days. We had no life jackets, no radios, and hurricane warnings came over crackling transistor radios. The old fishers knew the signs, of course, the way dawn broke, the way the swells ran, how the birds flew. They would pull their boats high on the beach and they would wait. They were not always right.

The Pedro fishers brought home bounty—hundreds of pounds of fish—grouper and red snapper and parrot. They sold their fish in Kingston and with the money they made, they bought land in Treasure Beach. They bought herds of goats. The inside fishers thrived too and the Calabash Bay market expanded. The fishing beaches thrummed with activity—boats being repaired, boats being readied for sea, boats coming home. Luke and I earned money scrubbing the mossy hulls of boats with sand.

My brothers went to Pedro in twos. We went to see them off and we waited for their return. Our father did not go. He had made the trip from Complex in his time, but he said it was now time for his sons to go. He was by then using a spear gun on the reefs near the coastline of our parish, St. Elizabeth, and his catches were good. Most fishers could not swim but my father had at one time been a lifeguard for a Montego Bay hotel—he was the best swimmer in Great Bay. He taught us to swim when we were very young—I do not remember a time when I could not swim.

The first time Ben and Lewis went to Pedro, our mother left the house. We had heard her speaking to our father the previous night in a new voice. I know we must have heard the words themselves—the house was small, though the walls were thick—but I do not remember them. We knew she hated the idea and she did not return until my brothers had gone, after midnight. There was no dinner that night. We ate the remains of a roasted breadfruit, left on the coal pot from the previous day. Next morning, I saw the groove between her eyebrows was deep.

My brothers went in a four-boat convoy to the Pedro Bank. It was late when they left and I thought the night was darker than usual. We stood on the beach and watched them go. The boats made a ragged triangle formation, like a flock of birds, and for a few seconds, their wakes were visible. Then they pierced the night and disappeared. The lead boat was Resurrection, *the captain was an old fisher called Maas Jerome, who spent three months at a time on Top Cay on the Bank. He was considered a good man to go to sea with. I stared into the moonless night, the stars hidden by clouds, but it was too dark to see anything. We could hear the boat engines although we could no longer see any sign of them and it was a final, ebbing connection to land. I stepped closer to my father. Why them don't take a light with them, Dada? I said.*

Close you eyes, he said and I obeyed him. Keep them closed. I stood on the beach and jumped when a wave ran over my toes, but I kept my eyes shut. I heard the sea, falling and rising and falling. Now open you eyes, my father said.

I looked and I saw familiar shapes become visible. If you take a light to sea, you can't see inna the dark, my father said. A man at sea need him night sight.

How they will find their way back? I said.

The lighthouse, my father said. The one at Lover's Leap. I thought about going to sea on a dark night with the only point of reference being a slim sweeping blade of light on a cliff behind me. The story goes that slave lovers jumped to their death from that cliff rather than be separated.

My brothers returned three weeks later. They were thin and their skins looked crisp, like a fish fried too long. They went straight to where we washed and they used bucket after bucket of fresh water. Then they went to bed and they slept for almost a day. They did not seem hungry. They did not speak much about what they had seen, not at first, or what it was like out at Pedro, but they brought back both money and fish, big fat snappers and groupers, the likes of which were already becoming rare around Great Bay. They talked of going again. And so Luke and I wanted to see for ourselves. We wanted to take the long journey to the Pedro Bank. We told ourselves we would be men, fishermen, if we took that ride.

7

"Where you think you going yout'?" said the security guard at the Morgan's Harbour Hotel. He sat in a little white building and lifted the red and white barrier up and down for cars. Lloyd had simply ducked under it, not seeing the guard until too late. He stopped.

"Mornin," he said, hoping a respectful politeness would win the guard over. "Me meetin somebody. She say me should wait for her under that almond tree." He pointed.

"What the name of the person?

"Jules-somethin. Just meet her, over at the fishing beach."

"So where she is? She on a boat? How you meet her if she on a boat? You should know her last name, so it can write up inna the book."

"Not a boat. Surfboard. She soon come, man. Me will just wait over there, under the tree. You can see me. Me not going move from there."

"Can't let you in yout'. Not without the person full name for the book. Step back."

Lloyd looked at the guard. He was young, in his twenties. His uniform was not properly ironed and he wore cheap dark glasses, the kind sold by downtown vendors. His hands were rough with big knuckles. Perhaps he had been a construction worker and had found easier work as a security guard and was not going to lose his job over a strange boy.

Lloyd stepped back, ducked under the barrier, and stood on the side of the Palisadoes Road, looking around for a place to wait. He needed to see the entrance to the hotel as he was afraid that the woman would not come right out into the parking lot, but would simply stand on the front step and look for him under the almond tree. If he was not there, she would turn around and go back into the hotel and he might never find her again. There was a little shade beside the gate but it gave no clear view of the front door. Lloyd crossed the road and stood in the sun, waiting for the dolphin woman.

He did not wait long—she could make that surfboard move fast-fast. As he had thought, she walked out of the hotel, stood on the curb and looked toward the almond tree. She shrugged and turned to go back inside. "Hi! Miss!" he called, as he had done from the dock. "Over here!" A bus drove past just then with a line of cars behind it, and he could not cross the road. She might not hear him or see him. "Miss!" he shouted to her back, jumping up and down, trying to be seen over the cars.

"That her?" said the guard, coming out of his shelter.

"Yes! Please, sah, please? Let me in. Do. Please." Lloyd was finally able to run across the road. He waved his arms, hoping the movement would catch the woman's eye. He could barely see her now—the inside of the hotel was in deep shadow. "MISS!" he shouted one last time, and the woman came out of the hotel into the parking lot.

"What . . . ?" she said. She shook her head and said something under her breath. She walked over to the barrier. She was wearing rolled up jeans over her wet suit and a towel around her neck. "He's with me," she said to the guard and her voice was sharp.

The guard was not impressed. "What him name and your name?"

"You write up my name already. You don't remember? Look in the book. Jules Collier. His name is Lloyd."

"Need him last name."

"Saunders," Lloyd said. See! He wanted to say to the guard. He was sweating more than ever in his church clothes. He wiped his face on his sleeve. The guard wrote slowly in his big register.

"Come inside, Lloyd," Jules said. "I need to change. We can get you a drink and you can tell me your story."

They sat at a bar overlooking Kingston Harbour. Lloyd had never been inside the hotel although from the sea he had seen the bar and the masts of sailboats moored in the marina. The seawater pool was murky and seaweed grew on its sides. He could not imagine white people swimming in it. He saw no guests although many tables were set for lunch with bandanna tablecloths and white napkins and empty glasses.

"What you want to drink?" Jules said, as the bartender stood in front of them.

"Soda, Miss."

"Which kind? Pepsi? Coke? Ting? Ginger beer?"

"Pepsi."

"A Pepsi and a Ting," Jules said. "They on ice? You hungry, Lloyd? You want anything to eat?"

"Kitchen not open 'til twelve," said the bartender.

"You don't have any bar snacks?"

"Cheese crunchies, plantain chips . . ."

"Two each," she said. "Plenty ice with the drinks."

When the drinks came, Jules got up and moved to one of the tables nearer to the dock. The wind was strong and Lloyd felt less noticeable. If he were to leave the table, if he were to walk over and sit on the dock, with his back to the hotel, if he narrowed his eyes and gazed out to sea, he could pretend he was on the dock of the Port Royal fishing beach and no one would come and tell him to move.

A man washed down the decks of the nearest large boat, flying an American flag. Lloyd wondered what it would be like to go to sea on a boat like that—he could see tables and upholstered seats through the hatchway. He wondered if they needed crew, if they fished, or if they just moved around from place to place, marina to marina. What would it be like to own such a vessel, to truly live on the sea?

". . . your story?" Lloyd realized Jules was talking to him. He took a sip of his drink and it was so cold it hurt his teeth and he could not really taste it. She pushed two of the bags of snacks over to him and opened one for herself.

"So tell me," she said. "What happen to your granddaddy?"

"He go to Pedro. Sunday night. Leave from Rocky Point. Him don't fish at Pedro. Never. Him was supposed to reach back Thursday, but him don't come back."

"When last you heard from him?"

"Wednesday."

"Him went alone?"

"Dunno, Miss. Nobody at Gray Pond beach seen him. The fishers say to ask the Coast Guard; they say they go out there every Monday night. Me come over here to see if they will look for him. One time, a boat from the Yacht Club don't come back and the Coast Guard did go out, and even the JDF send up a helicopter, and them found the boat wrecked down by Hellshire, and them found the men too, in life jackets. Dead." Lloyd stopped. He did not want the JDF to find his grandfather's wrecked boat, or his body. "Gramps, mebbe his boat engine give out. Mebbe him on a beach somewhere, can't get back. Me just want somebody to look for him."

Jules ran her hands over her hair. "I don't know if the JDF will look for him, Lloyd. But is true, a Coast Guard boat go out to Pedro once a week. They take men out and bring men back; maybe they will ask some questions. Give me a minute to shower and change and make us go over there and ask them."

"Them will take me with them to Pedro? Me can find him, Miss. Me know him is out there somewhere. Sea can't kill my granddaddy."

Jules shook her head. "I don't think they will take you. But let's ask. Soon come. You just sit here, eat up. Sorry is not better food, maybe we can get some fish in Port Royal after." She got up, left her drink on the table and most of the cheese crunchies uneaten, and walked around the dining room behind them. Lloyd felt the bartender's gaze. He was sure the bartender thought the likes of him should not be allowed to sit at a table at the Morgan's Harbour Hotel.

He waited. He was anxious, sitting there alone, and he hoped Jules would come back quickly. He did not know how to talk to her. He wanted to ask her about her work with dolphins. Was she a scientist? He had seen scientists working in the Port Royal mangroves, with their wide-brimmed hats, their clipboards and rolls of tape. He did not know what they did there, but he saw them writing and taking pictures.

He knew the mangroves as a place where it was safe to moor a boat when a hurricane threatened, that somehow the sea remained much calmer inside their lagoons and channels. Many kinds of bird lived there—old joes, terns, gulls, herons—and some types of fish hid among the roots. He liked the strange shoots that grew downward from the plants. The strong smell of the swamp did not bother him.

If Maas Conrad was late coming back from sea, he always went into a channel through the mangroves to a place called Rosey's Hole, where the leaves almost touched overhead and it was shady and quiet. Gramps would sling a line around one of the trees and pull the boat in close and there he would eat a bulla and an overripe pear and drink a hot Red Stripe beer. Sometimes he would lie back in the boat and sleep, while Lloyd slapped at mosquitoes and watched fallen leaves drift past.

They would motor out, as slowly as possible, so as not to send big waves surging through the mangroves, disrupting the order of

and Gramps would get upset when he saw garbage tangled up in

roots and he would tell Lloyd it would affect the fishing, but he didn't

say how. He always said "fish-nin" instead of "fish-ing." Lloyd thought

Jules probably knew about mangroves and why they might affect fish-

nin.

"You ready?" she said, from behind him. He got up. She was

carrying her surfboard and paddle under one arm and held a backpack

in the other. "Let's go. Don't want you to get your hopes up, though—I

don't know if Commander Peterson is even going to be there. But

make us go and see what we can see."

Her car was an old Jeep with a canvas top. She loaded the surfboard

in the back and tied a red cloth to it to show where it stuck out. "Get

in," she said and there was a touch of impatience in her voice. Perhaps

she was already sorry she had talked to him, perhaps she wished she

could just take him back to the dock in Port Royal.

It took them less than a minute to get to the Coast Guard station.

The gate was the cut off top of an old ship called the HMJS *Cagway*

and there was a sign saying the base had been founded in 1963. The rmed guard obviously knew Jules and smiled as she drove up to

guard post. "Commander here?" she asked.

"Him on *Surrey*," said the guard. "But you can wait for him." He

didn't seem to notice Lloyd.

"Awright, Phillips, thanks. Park in the usual place?" Jules didn't

wait for an answer.

They drove along a narrow road beside the Harbour. The Coast

Guard base was a mix of new buildings and old—crumbling red brick

and square concrete buildings. He saw a line of long wooden houses

painted blue off to the left. They all had signs with the names of sea

creatures—Shark, Barracuda, Dolphin.

She parked under a large willow tree. She turned to Lloyd and

looked at him. "Let me do the talking, okay? What you granddaddy

name again?"

"Conrad. Maas Conrad Saunders."

They walked along a pathway toward the dock. Everything was very

neat and painted, even the trunks of the coconut trees. The grass

was brown and mowed. There was not a trace of litter. Lloyd could

faintly hear the noise of some kind of machinery, perhaps a drill or a generator. They passed men in uniform, light blue shirts and dark blue trousers, who nodded to Jules and said, "Miss." They passed a line of old willow trees, all leaning in one direction, making a soft sound in the sea breeze. They walked past an old concrete jetty, almost at sea level, covered with seagulls, also facing in one direction.

They walked onto the dock. The three big Coast Guard boats were moored together—the *Surrey* on one side of the dock, the *Cornwall* on the other, and the *Middlesex* tied up to the *Cornwall*. Two scuba divers were in the water at the stern of the *Surrey*, apparently cleaning the hull and propellers. Lloyd saw there was a stern ladder into the sea.

"We wait for him here," Jules said and she walked to the end of the dock and sat, her legs dangling over the side, leaning back on her arms. She was wearing a clean pair of jeans, a white T-shirt, and the kind of buckled sandals that you could wear in the sea and were good on boats. Her skin was dark against the white T-shirt. She stared at the Harbour and swung her legs. She seemed fine in the hot sun and Lloyd wished he was wearing shorts and an undershirt. His shoes pinched. Behind them, sailors were lined up in rows doing drills of some kind. He smelled melting asphalt. No one challenged them.

Jules seemed entirely at home on the Coast Guard base.

He sat beside her, but not too close. How to talk to her? How old was she? Twenty, he thought, maybe twenty-one, but then he remembered how easily she spoke with the guard at the Coast Guard gate, and the expert way she had handled the dolphin on Lime Cay. If she was a scientist, she would have been to university. Maybe she was twenty-five. Was she from Kingston? Did she still live in the city? What was she doing with the Coast Guard and why did they know her well enough to allow her onto the base? Did she ever fish? Had she been to the Pedro Cays? Could he trust her? He had no idea how to frame his questions. He feared they might seem disrespectful and she would be offended, but he thought it would be okay to ask about the Cays. "You been to Pedro, Miss?" he said.

"Many times," she said. "At least once a month."

"Why? You fishing out there?" As Lloyd said it, he knew how ridiculous the idea was. A woman fishing! Women were the cleaners and sellers of fish; men were the ones who brought them out of the sea.

Jules smiled. "Sometimes, if I want to eat a fish, I catch one. But no, I'm not out there fishing. I'm taking a census of dolphins on the

Bank—counting—trying to find out how many there are, what species—what kinds—of dolphins."

"How you do that?"

"Go out in a boat. We have a big map, where we draw out squares in the sea, then we go up and down in a pattern. If we see a dolphin we take a picture of his dorsal fin, put it in a computer, so we make sure we don't count the same one twice. Just look for them and count."

Lloyd could not imagine the drawing of squares in the sea. "You see a lot of them?" he asked.

She shrugged. "Depends on what you mean by a lot. Not compared to the amount that was probably there in old-time days. But more than I expected to find, yes. Mostly bottlenose. Some white-sided. Seen killer whales too—you know them?"

Lloyd shook his head; he had never heard of a killer whale. They sounded dangerous, not at all like dolphins.

"You seen *Free Willy*?"

"No, Miss. What is *Free Willy*?

"A movie about a killer whale. I bet you seen a picture of one—they're black and white, like a panda."

Lloyd did not want to ask what a panda was but he wanted Jules to keep talking. "Why you countin up the dolphins?"

"Want to know if the population is healthy. How many animals. If they are breeding; things like that."

"Why you don't do it close to shore? Pedro Cays far."

Jules nodded. "Far, yes. But not so many dolphins inshore these days, too little food for them to eat. Not enough fish. Your granddaddy probably know about that. There's a place out at Pedro, a bare rock, deep water around, nice reefs. We see a lot of dolphins there."

"You went to school to study about dolphins?"

"Four years," she said. "In California."

"Why?"

"Why did I want to study dolphins?" She shrugged again. "Grew up beside the sea in Portie. Always loved it. Saw an angry fisher spear a dolphin once, the dolphin was fooling around with his trap. I thought it was a smart animal, to try and get the fish out. So I went to college in the US to learn about them."

Lloyd's eyes suddenly filled with tears. He did not want to talk about dolphins. He wanted to talk about Gramps, about his fears for the old man, his fears for himself. Who would speak kindly to him if his grandfather was never seen again? Who would teach him about manhood, about life? He wished for his grandfather's low, rough voice, telling him dolphin stories, or about how the fish-nin was good, so good, in the old days. He had thought some of his stories boring, now he wanted to hear them all, again and again.

He knew his voice would shake if he spoke and he did not want the woman to hear that. He had to be strong. He said nothing. The sun was directly overhead and he wanted to find shade but he thought of Gramps lost at sea with the sun like a hammer on his head. So he closed his eyes and saw the sun bright inside his eyelids, as Gramps would, wherever he was. And he stayed where he was, on the dock at Cagway base, keeping company with his lost grandfather.

On this rock where now I lie, the sea snails are salty but easy to pull off the rocks and crack open. I eat three every time the sun has moved the span of my hand. Then I get up and look to the horizon and think of the line drawn in my young life: the before and the after, the time before Luke went to sea and the time after.

How it go? I asked Luke after his first trip.

Hard, was all he said. Me sleep on mesh wire.

Another day he said, There was a man with two rows of teeth, like a shark.

And another day: Good. Fish was biting.

And, When you see the bluff you know you are home. Even before that you can smell the land.

After Luke went to sea, there were many mornings when I was the only boy in the house. When he and Lewis left the bed we shared, half asleep I would change my position, move from the bottom of the bed to put my head on the only pillow and stretch out my limbs. The nights were often hot and the tangle of boy limbs sweaty and full of hard angles. When the others left, I fell into a deep and undisturbed sleep. My mother would wake me and ask if I planned to sleep the day away. It was a luxury, to sleep in such comfort, but it was lonely too, and when I woke, I hardly knew what to do with myself.

I had been left at home, in the world of women. I felt a small knot of anger under my breast bone, like a dried almond, hidden in the sand. I spoke to the Arawak prince in my mind. If only I had been born a prince. I wanted to name him. I asked our teacher, Miss Carlton, about the Arawaks and she sent me to one of the dusty encyclopedia volumes on a shelf in the tiny, nearly empty room that was called a library. She read out loud about a chief called Hatuey from Hispaniola, who led a rebellion in Cuba and was burned alive. I named my prince after him.

The water level in the plastic bottle is going down too quickly—I must be more careful. I find a new pool with a few whelks—much bigger than the sea snails, but their thick black and white shells are harder to crack. I long for a tool, any tool. I find a cavity in the rocks that is a little smaller than a whelk and I wedge one there and hit it with the sharpest rock I can find, trying to hit the same spot with every blow. Breaking the shell takes a long time and while I hit the whelk I wonder how it made its way to this rock in the sea with deep water all around. There were many whelks in Treasure Beach when I was a boy and sometimes my mother made whelk soup. She put the broken shells along our fence line, made with wild coffee sticks, and the shiny insides of the shells glistened in the sun.

The whelk's shell breaks. I scrape off the bits of shell with my fingernails, taking my time, and when I put it in my mouth, it feels as meaty as a good oxtail. I must ration the little colony of whelks—I will eat one per day when the sun is at its highest. But the need for fresh water is now urgent. I search the sky for rain clouds but the sky is clear. I search the sea but there are still no fishing boats.

8

They waited almost an hour. Jules seemed comfortable on the dock although she did take a baseball cap out of her backpack and put it on, apologizing because she only had one hat. Lloyd saw there was a quietness about her; a patience, a willingness to wait as long as was necessary. Maybe this came from studying the sea. Fishing needed patience too. He wondered what she would have been doing if he had not called to her from the Port Royal dock. He watched her out of the corner of his eye. She sat braced against her hands, her legs moving back and forth, and he longed for her patience. All the same, it is not her grandfather lost, he thought. Maybe she would be on the *Surrey* already if it was her grandfather.

A ray jumped in front of them and she said, "Spotted ray. Bottom feeder. Lot of them live in the Harbour." Lloyd thought all rays were stingrays. He wished he knew as much as she did about the sea. Did she know more than Gramps? She studied dolphins, but did she love them? Would she believe Gramps's stories about dolphins helping people?

He gazed at the *Surrey*, moored to their right. The end of the dock was about two thirds of the way along the ship's length. Jules had said he would not be allowed to go to Pedro, but maybe there was a way to get on board. The *Surrey* was large in comparison to a canoe, but it was not that high. He thought he could climb aboard on a rope. The weather rail that lined the deck was solid gray steel, but it had square holes with rounded edges along its length, and there was a hole at the prow of the ship where the anchor rope went through. Lloyd thought he could fit through any of the holes.

It was harder to imagine what he would do once on deck and he had no idea what was below deck. He could see an open hatch on the forward deck, into which the anchor rope disappeared. He thought about the coiled anchor rope of *Water Bird*, under her bow cap, and the way Gramps stowed things he did not want to get wet, right up against the V of the prow. He could still easily fit inside that small triangle.

Perhaps there was a hiding place where the anchor rope of the *Surrey* was stored. Lloyd saw two men on the flying bridge watching them.

Behind the men, a uniformed sailor stood at a gap in the weather rail—a sentry, he assumed, there to stop people like himself from boarding. The two men on the bridge climbed down the ladder to the lower deck and approached the sentry, who saluted and pointed to where they sat. Jules stood. "That's him," she said, her arm held up, in the salute of the sea. One of the men walked up to her. "Jules?" he said. "Did I forget an appointment?"

"No, man," she said, smiling. The flash of her teeth illuminated her whole face. "Just came over on spec. This is Lloyd Saunders. Lloyd, Commander Peterson."

"Lloyd," said Commander Peterson. He looked at his watch. "I have a meeting at fourteen hundred hours," he said to Jules. "What's up?"

"Lloyd's grandfather went to Pedro last Sunday, but hasn't come back. We were wondering if your guys could ask around out there—you going out tomorrow night as usual?"

"Yes. About midnight. Captain Blake will be in command. Sure, no problem. He can ask around, but why don't we just radio the base on Middle Cay? What's your grandfather's name?" he said to Lloyd.

"Maas Conrad, sah," Lloyd said. "Conrad Saunders."

"Him have a pet name?

"No, Maas Conrad is what them call him."

"Him is a regular Pedro fisher? Don't recognize the name."

"No, sah. Him don't go Pedro. Him more go California Banks, Bowditch. But him go Pedro last Sunday and him don't come back." Lloyd gathered his courage. He did not think radioing the Pedro base would work. "Me can go with the boat, sah? Me can find him. Me can crew if you want."

The Commander laughed. "No, Lloyd, I'm sorry, but that can't work. But don't worry, my men will ask around. They know everybody on Pedro and if anybody out there knows anything, they will find out."

"When they will be back, sah?"

"Boat turns around overnight. Goes out, takes out the new crew, brings back the men out there."

"The boat don't stay out there?"

77

"No. Goes out, comes back. Only a few hours out there, anchored off Middle Cay. You can check us Wednesday, late afternoon. Depends on the weather. I will radio out there now, get the men to start asking a few questions. The weather is not looking that good midweek, so—"

"But—" Lloyd said.

Jules put her hand on his shoulder. "Thanks, Commander. Appreciate your help. If you hear anything, call me."

"Your men will look out for him on the sea?" Lloyd said, despite Jules's hand, warning him to be quiet and grateful. He knew the crew of the *Surrey* would be able to see much farther across the sea than the crew of a fishing canoe. Maybe they would see a boat with a dead engine in the swell and fall of the waves.

"My men always keep a good watch, son," said Commander Peterson, and Lloyd heard the edge in his voice.

That night, he went again to the seawall after his mother was asleep. She seemed not to have noticed his disappearance all day. Boys were expected to be unruly and Lloyd knew it was enough for her that he returned home for the evening meal—that night a hearty chicken soup, made from chicken neck and back, with yam and cho cho and large solid dumplings. He had been hungry—Jules had forgotten her promise of fish at Gloria's so his lunch had consisted of the snacks he had eaten at the Morgan's Harbour Hotel. As they ate in silence, Lloyd knew his mother had something on her mind.

After the visit to the Coast Guard base, Jules had driven him to Gray Pond beach at his request—he had not wanted her to see where he lived. She had asked how to find him if she heard anything about Maas Conrad, and he told her that anyone at Gray Pond would know where to find him. He had watched the Jeep drive away and he felt alone. He had not even said thanks and he had not found out where to find her. She had said he should not worry about Gramps, but he felt her words were empty. Another day done and there was still no news of his grandfather.

The hot night was cloudy and the sky hung low. It was the middle of the hurricane season. There could be a storm at any time. The words *any time* had two meanings. His grandfather could return at any time, but also a storm could blow up any time, a storm that would sink a lost fishing canoe in the first half hour. The Coast Guard commander was right; the weather was changing. A storm was out there. He leaned against the light pole and thought about the *Surrey*. There must be places on board where a small boy could hide. Surely the sailors would not do anything bad to a small boy when he was found, especially if the small boy was only seeking news of his grandfather. He wished he could wait for a trip when Jules would be there, but it was clear she had no plans to go to Pedro the next day.

The problem was how to get on board the ship. He was sure there would always be a sentry at the entry port. The stern ladder was very close to the dock so he knew he could swim to the ship from the Port Royal fishing beach—he could hug the coast and move through the water as silently as any large fish. But then what? Could he climb the anchor rope onto the deck and disappear into the anchor well? He thought he might be able to, and if he failed, all that would happen was he would fall into the sea. He thought of the jumping ray—he would sound like a ray hitting the water, no one would notice.

But once on deck, he would be exposed. Could he climb the stern ladder and find a hiding place there? He was sorry he had not asked the commander if he could tour the ship. He could have pretended to be a boy in love with ships, and maybe the commander would have showed him around with pride. He could have made a better plan then.

Lloyd knew the word "stowaway"—occasionally people from other countries, Haiti in particular, stowed away on the ships that came into Kingston Harbour. When they were found, they were arrested and taken away. It was risky, dangerous even, but he made his decision. He would try to be a stowaway on the *Surrey*. The anchor rope or the stern ladder? He stared into the night and worried over his plans.

My time to go to sea came and I wanted to be alone with my father for my first journey, but Luke was there. I complained and my father cuffed the side of my head. Watch you mout', bwoy, he said. After that we worked in silence in the dark. I was afraid but full of anticipation too. The first trip was never to the Pedro Bank—that would come later—but would we go out so far that there would be no sign of land? How would we find our way back in the day, without the shining lighthouse?

What I can still see from that first trip: the sunrise. It had been a night of fast-moving clouds, the moon just past full. The sea shone in the moonlight. The only sound was the throb of the engine. Luke stood in the bow, I sat facing forward. Our father stood behind me with his hand on the tiller. How did he know where to go?

We motored for what seemed like an age, but was probably only an hour. Then I realized I could see my hands and feet as a gray light stole across the sea. And to the east I saw the sky turning into a hundred different colors—from the blue of a summer day to the dark purple of the thickest squall, from the pale pink of the inside of a conch shell to the bright orange of a ripe mango, until the round ball of the sun itself came up and the colors of the sky spread over the water and even warmed our faces. I knew then that the best place to see a sunrise was at sea.

When the sun came up, I saw it was the same sea I knew and my nervous anticipation left me. After that, it was just a long learning of all the things my brothers had already learned: the gear, the methods, the times and places of a fisherman. I absorbed this learning with ease, it was nothing like the torture of a school desk, of chalk and blackboard; this was a learning of the body, of all the senses. My father hardly spoke to us; he showed us what to do. This way, he would say. Sit beside me and take the tiller. You see that over there, that funny flat cloud? Time to run for home.

That first morning, the best thing I saw was the dolphins.

9

Lloyd got up at fishing time. He had hardly slept. He had to get out of
the house before his mother woke—she would not let him miss another
day's selling. He wrote her a note saying he was crewing for a fisher
nicknamed Popeye; he was not sure when he would be back, but he
would be home with money. He knew his mother might go to Gray
Pond beach to speak to Maas Benjy or Maas Rusty, but he hoped she
would not do it until the next day and by then he would be long gone.

He had thought about the trip for most of the night. He had no
idea how long the Coast Guard boat would take to get to the Pedro
Cays so he had packed a bottle of water in his school bag and three
bullas from the food cupboard. He had put a cap, his rag, and a
change of clothes in a plastic bag to keep them dry. He counted his
money. He would need another plastic bag for that. He dressed in his

fishing clothes—the torn up ones in the darkest colors—they would not stand out in the night as he tried to find a hiding place. Then he looked at the bag and shook his head: fool-fool. He had to swim to the boat and then climb up a rope and through a small hole—how could he take a bag with him? Could he put the whole bag in another plastic bag? Could he find an old piece of Styrofoam and float the bag along with him? He thought that was worth trying and if he mashed up his school bag, he had more than a month to find a new one before school started again.

He spent the day on Princess Street among the vendors. It was one of the most crowded parts of downtown Kingston and he made his way unnoticed through the vendors' stalls on sidewalks and in the streets, past the jelly coconut men, the dry goods vendors, and the pan chicken cooks—you could buy anything in downtown Kingston—clothes, shoes, food, drugs, guns. He searched the narrow lanes between the wider streets and found a pile of cardboard and he went through it looking for Styrofoam. He was glad to be out of the sun. He found several plastic bags and the kind of bubbly plastic wrap that was used for packing; he remembered how he and Dwight had scared their teachers by popping the bubbles in the same kind of wrap at the back of their classroom. Even a small noise could make a teacher spin around in a Kingston primary school, fearing gunshots.

He wished Dwight was coming with him. This day and night would be an adventure then, a prank, like the time they rowed Maas Braham's dinghy around the point at Gray Pond beach and hid it behind some sea grape trees. He found a long roll of twine—part of it plastered with dog doo-doo. He unrolled the twine and used his pocket knife to cut away the dirtiest part. He could now tie up his plastic bag and maybe his clothes would be kept dry. He did not find anything that would float. By noon, he was longing to drink from his store of water but he resisted. His hands were filthy and, like his grandfather wherever he was, he knew he would have to use his supplies slowly.

He found a standpipe but it was dry. He bought suck-suck and a boiled corn from a vendor and he walked toward the waterfront. He sat in the shade of a coconut tree and ate his lunch, taking care not to touch the corn with his dirty hands. He thought again about climbing onto the *Surrey* and his hopefulness left him. It would never work. It was too much for a boy, small for his age, a boy who did downgrow, according to his mother. He threw the suck-suck plastic bag into the Harbour and immediately heard his grandfather's voice in his mind: Turtle going think that a jellyfish.

There was a parking lot nearby. He watched the security guard at the entrance and the comings and goings of drivers and vehicles. There was a group of men skylarking on a small mound of uncut grass at the edge of the parking lot farthest away from the entrance. He saw the security guard watching them, his attention divided between motorists and the men. Then one of Kingston's many homeless men ran across the two-lane road right in front of an oncoming car. The car's brakes screeched and the noise pulled everyone's gaze, including the guard's. The homeless man was safe on the median strip, but he began a loud cursing.

As Lloyd watched, he saw one of the men on the grassy mound take a long metal strip from the grass, jump down into the parking lot, fit the strip into the window of the nearest car and, in a few seconds, open the door. He took something out of the car—Lloyd could not see what—shut the car door and went back to his bredren. Lloyd knew the guard had not seen what had happened and later, when the loss of the car owner's property was reported, he would swear it could not have taken place on his shift. That's what I need, he realized. Something to make the sailors look away while I climb the rope. He would have to find Dwight.

It was Luke who saw them first. My father was tinkering with the engine, there was a sputtering noise he did not like. Look, Luke said, and pointed. I saw a splashing in the water near the reef but it was too far away to see what was causing it—it could have been any school of large fish. Dolphins, my father said, looking up from the outboard.

We went slowly over to the reef, my father taking Silver *through the rocks and coral heads. When we were still some distance away, he cut the engine and tilted it forward over the stern so the propeller was no longer in the sea. That way we could cross over the reef wherever there was two feet of water without grounding the boat. We glided. And then right beside us, clear against the sandy seafloor, I saw the gray shape of what I took to be a shark. Shark, I said. And then the gray shape came to the surface with the same sound I made after I dived down for a conch and held my breath too long. Dolphin, said my father. Not shark. Dolphin go up and down at the surface, shark swim straight. I saw the dolphin's dorsal fin go up and down and then it dived and then they were all around us.*

Now, I am not sure what enchanted me. Yes, they were big, bigger than most animals we were used to seeing. Yes, they had smiling faces and bright eyes. But I think it was the way they seemed to be playing in the sea that caused me to remain staring down into the water long after they had gone, hoping they would return.

Pass the oar, my father said. Not yet, I wanted to say, but I remained silent. There was work to be done. He had just been humoring me on my first trip as a fisher. He pushed us off the reef and when we were in deeper water he started the engine and we began to pull my father's fish pots. Whenever we rested, I stared at the place where the dolphins had made their splashing and wished there was some way of marking it, so I could be sure I could find it again.

I left one swallow of water in the plastic bottle last night and this morning it is gone. I don't know if I left the top open a little and it leaked out or if I imagined the tiny amount of water. I stare out to sea and I think I see rain clouds. I sit and watch them, willing them to me. My head wound is better but one of the cuts on my right leg hurts. It is getting harder and harder to stand.

10

Lloyd found Dwight at Victoria Pier casting a line into Kingston Harbour, a bucket on the beach for his catch. "Yow, bredren," he called out to his friend.

"Wha'ppen Lloydie? How come you not sellin uptown?"

"Need to do sumpn. Want you help."

"What you want?"

"Come over here and me tell you."

Dwight reeled in his line and splashed through the shallow water to where Lloyd stood on the beach. "Whoy! Why you smell so, bredren?"

"Just dog doo-doo on this twine me find. Me soon wash it off."

"What you want?"

"Gramps still don't come home. Me want hide on the Coast Guard boat, go out to Pedro with them, see if me can find him."

"What!? You turn fool, bredren? Them nah going let you on that boat!"

"Listen me. Me going climb the anchor rope. Or the stern ladder. Me need you to do sumpn so them all look at you while me is doin it."

"But see here now. Lloydie, you not thinkin straight. Can't work, trust me. Can't work."

"Dwight. You comin or you not? Me gettin on a bus and me going to Port Royal and me going wait for night, and then me is going to climb that rope and get on the boat. If them catch me, them catch me. Me going to try."

"Whoy," Dwight said again. Then he smiled. "Well, is you them going throw inna jail. What you want me do?"

The rain clouds come. The weather always changes if you wait long enough. I crawl out from under the shade of the blue tarpaulin and the rain washes salt and blood from my skin. I drink. The hollows in the rocks around me fill with fresh water. Perhaps I now have a store of water for days. I forget the cuts in my back from the rocks and the pain in my right leg. I abandon my rationing and eat dozens of sea snails. There are only five whelks left. I open my mouth to the sky, rain fills my body and I feel strength fill my arms. I crack the biggest remaining whelk easily—I have learned the best place to hit their tough shells. I make a funnel of the tarpaulin and fill the plastic bottle, wishing I had another container. I taste the water in one of the rock pools but it is brackish. I realize the rocks hold millennia of salt from the sea and they cannot be washed clean.

Five days I have been on this rock. With water I can survive five more. I stand and turn a slow circle, searching for the horizon but it is hidden behind sheets of rain. Then the whole world seems to turn and I fall to my knees.

It rains for hours and hours and I mourn the wasted water that falls into the sea. When the rain stops, my skin dries quickly and I watch the sun sink into a bank of cloud. That night I have no dreams.

11

The boys sat right at the back of the bus and Lloyd stared out of the window. Where could they wait until dark? Port Royal was a small town and they would be recognized if they went to the fishing beach. Then Lloyd remembered a ruined fort he had seen from Lime Cay; he had never been there on land, but it was close to Port Royal. They would try to find it.

The bus turned onto the new road of the Palisadoes strip with the huge stones piled up by Chinese engineers to make a seawall. He saw the sea was rough. It was going to be an uncomfortable journey to Pedro.

The boys got off the bus at the Morgan's Harbour Hotel and walked back in the direction they had come. Lloyd hoped the fort was not far; it was hard to tell distances from the sea. The sun beat down on his head and heat rose off the surface of the road. His bag had seemed light in the morning, but now the water bottle was heavy. He was dirty and tired and he had not yet boarded the *Surrey*.

The entrance to the fort was right on the main road. The site had recently been bushed and there was no one there. Lloyd led the way onto the beach—Lime Cay was straight ahead, swimming distance, if the currents were right. Although the sand was gray and hot, there was a strong breeze off the sea and it cooled the sweat on his skin. This was the place to wait looking out to Lime Cay where the uptowners went on weekends. Perhaps there would even be a pipe somewhere where he could wash the twine and his hands and face.

"It nice here," said Dwight, and Lloyd realized it was true. The coast curved into a shallow bay and the sea was calmer just in front of them. The beach was covered with rocks of all sizes and shapes and colors, most smooth, and where the waves broke, the stones made a clacking noise as the sea rushed in and out. There was a line of garbage at the edge of the sea, plastic bottles and old shoes and discarded fishing gear and various kinds of wood. Behind them the sand dunes were covered with sea grape and macca bushes and different kinds of cactus.

Lloyd knew the pretty sea had a secret. Whenever Gramps came in from fishing, he would take *Water Bird* so close to the same strip of land on which they stood that Lloyd often thought they would run aground. "Bottom drop off steep-steep," Gramps had said in explanation. "Man always drown here." If the boys waded into the sea, within a few steps they would be out of their depth and caught in a tearing current heading for Wreck Reef and the Hellshire coast.

"So what now?" Dwight said.

"Make us look for a place to wait and a pipe. Want clean this twine—them will smell me before them see me."

"No pipe out here, man. Nobody is here. Wash it in the sea."

"Sea too clean. Come. Make us look around."

The boys walked away from the beach and followed a short marl track into the fort. It was built around a courtyard—some of the walls were brick, others were a kind of crumbling concrete. There was an enormous spray-painted drawing of a gun on one of the concrete walls with the slogan, "Tek sleep and mark death!" The slogan was underlined with dripping red paint to look like blood.

Lloyd saw a small building under a straggly coconut tree. It was almost in the middle of the courtyard, and it looked like the shelters used by security guards all over the city. It had a new zinc roof and a modern door, which was closed. They walked over to it and saw a standpipe right nearby. Probably this was a place where a security guard was sent to look after the fort for the government people. Lloyd knew Port Royal was a very old place, once a rich, wicked town that had been sent to the bottom of the sea in a great earthquake.

Lloyd knelt in the shade and turned on the pipe. There was a good chance it would not work. But fresh water gushed out and he groaned. He cupped his hands and washed them over and over, wiping them on a patch of long grass, and then washing them again and again, scraping under his nails, until he could no longer smell doo-doo. Then he drank, and splashed water on his head and face. He sat with his back against the building and closed his eyes. He realized he would have to wash his hands all over again after he had dealt with the twine, but they had all afternoon.

"You tired, Lloydie?" said Dwight.

"Yeah man."

"You have food?"

"Only some bulla. Have to keep it for in the night."

"Watch me now. You stay here. Me going wash the twine in the sea. Don't make sense do it under the pipe; take too long. Then me going into Port Royal, find sumpn to eat, look around. Maybe swim round the point and look at the boat. See how far it is."

Lloyd heard the concern in his friend's voice and he wanted to cry. He kept his eyes closed. Tears always brought laughter and teasing. "Look for a piece of Styrofoam," he said to Dwight.

"What kinda Styrofoam?"

"Any kind. Not a lunch box. Biggish. Want float my bag over to the boat. Me tie the bag to the string. If me get up on deck, then me pull up the bag."

"You smart! Okay. No problem."

"You a star, man," Lloyd said, and his voice was thick.

"Soon come," Dwight said. "Me bring you some food. And the Styrofoam."

I remember that by the time Luke went to Pedro that first time, he and I had abandoned **Birdie**. By then we were crew for other fishers. By then I went to school only occasionally and sometimes Miss Carlton came to our front door to speak to my mother about this.

The days while Luke was gone were long. It was hurricane season, late September, which caused my mother to keep the radio on day and night. But there were no storms that month, in fact, I remember it as a calm September with a clear liquid daylong light. Is this a trick of memory? I do not know. But I do remember being annoyed at the good weather; all the more reason I could have gone with Luke, for the risk was low. I was bored. The inshore waters of Great Bay were now too small.

While Luke was gone, Sheldon's Bar got a small black and white TV. By then, some places in Treasure Beach had electricity. The TV programs started at six in the evening, but even in the day we asked Sheldon to turn it on so we could look at the striped test screen in awe, laughing when it flickered. We were amazed by the talking people and moving images in a box. People reading the news. Cartoons. I loved Mr. Magoo and Road Runner. Beep-beep, the boys said when they saw each other in the lanes. Sheldon's business thrived and he became a big man in Great Bay. He bought a fishing boat.

Luke returned. Like my brothers before him, his eyes were flat and tired, his skin salt encrusted. He slept. He ate. He shrugged when I asked him how it was. Your time soon come, he said.

We got television while you were gone, I said.

12

Lloyd woke. His shirt was soaked with sweat and his neck hurt. He had fallen asleep against the building—his sleepless nights had finally caught up with him. Where was his backpack? Had it been stolen? He saw it was right beside him. The shadow of the coconut tree was longer and the afternoon was ending. He must have slept for at least two hours. Where was Dwight?

He stood up, feeling cramped and sluggish. He washed his face and hands again and the fresh water was a gift. He picked up his bag and walked over to the beach. It was cooler but the breeze still blew and the sea was up. If he managed to climb onto the *Surrey*, if he found a hiding place and remained hidden for the long hours to the Pedro Bank, would he get seasick?

He had never been seasick in his life, but he had only ever been to sea in an open canoe—he knew it was different below decks in a big ship, where it was airless and there was no steady horizon to look at. Gramps had taught him how to do that. When the sea heaved and threw a small boat around, when the waves fell away, leaving the boat hanging in midair for a stomach-churning moment before it crashed into the trough that followed every wave—a fisher must stare at the horizon, even when it was lost in cloud or rain, must stare at the one steady straight line in a rough world of weather and salt water.

Lloyd sat on one of the larger stones and looked out past Lime Cay to the horizon. He knew Pedro was out there, somewhere to the south and west. He saw the much cleaner twine stretched out on the beach, anchored by stones along its length, where Dwight had left it. He turned his face to the setting sun. He was very hungry, but he was calm. Perhaps it would be a good thing to go to sea in the belly of the *Surrey* with an empty stomach. He would either make it, or he wouldn't. But he was going to try.

He heard footsteps behind him and he turned. Dwight walked into the site, carrying an old ice chest. He waved and broke into a slow jog. "Look what me find!" he said. "This better than Styrofoam, don't it?" Lloyd got up and took it from him. It had a hole on one side, but it would float and the hole was high enough that if he swam very slowly, his bag might almost stay dry. The chest was almost perfect for the task ahead. It was a good omen.

"Here," Dwight said. "Some fry fish." Lloyd clapped his friend on the shoulder. If he was sick later, he would have to cope.

The boys sat on the beach while Lloyd ate. "Found out a whole heap," said Dwight. "Bucked up Maas Garnet, you know him? One elder. Used to fish, but him old-old now. Anyway, now him selling coconut. Him go inside the base all the time—"

"You don't tell him anything?"

"No man. Me tell him me doin a project for school. Him say them load up the boat by 'bout ten o'clock. Him say plenty confusion while boat is loadin. Him say everybody go on board by about eleven and then the boat go out by midnight."

"Still need a way to make them look at sumpn else."

"Listen me. Two of we swim over there. You wait on the starboard side—away from the dock—nobody watch that side. Then me go to the side where them is loadin up and me start shout and carry on and say me want come with them. While that going on, you climb the rope. Argument done."

"Them go think you mad," Lloyd said. "Them might arrest you."

"Me go on like me get hold of a bottle of white rum. Me dive back into the sea. Them nah come after me."

It was a simple plan, but it had a chance of working. Lloyd looked into his friend's face—his eyes were bright and he was smiling—he thought it was a game, like many they had played. "We not pickney anymore," he warned. He wanted Dwight to know what was at stake. Dwight shrugged.

"You think Gramps is awright?" Lloyd asked.

Dwight stopped smiling. "I dunno man. He could be, but I dunno. Is good you go look for him."

"Me wrote on a paper at home that me crewin for Popeye. If my mother ask, that's what you tell her, okay?"

"Yeah man. Me don't see you since Sunday. Where you want wait? Here or close to Port Royal?"

"Here. On the beach. The security might come back. See that tree?

Make us sit under it. Don't make me fall asleep again."

"Awright. Memba the twine." Lloyd unpacked the bigger plastic bag and stowed his backpack inside it, shoving it tight against the hole in the ice chest. The backpack fit perfectly. He walked along the beach, coiling the twine between palm and elbow; it still had a faint smell, but nothing came off on his hands. The boys crawled under the low branches of a sea grape tree and began their wait for nightfall.

I was not yet thirteen when I left school. Luke and I started fishing with other fishers, sometimes making two or three trips in a day. The bed I slept in with my two brothers was far too small and I moved to a rough, heavy blanket on the floor. I was fourteen, then fifteen. All I desired was a girlfriend so I went to sea as much as I could—I would need some money to catch a girl.

The one I really liked, Jasmine, was from Billy's Bay and the white blouse she wore under her school tunic was starched. She wore her hair in plaits, held by elastic bands with round balls at the ends. Sometimes her head was covered with these balls because her mother had made so many plaits. They reminded me of a thin cactus that bloomed round yellow balls once a year in June. I took Jasmine's hairstyle to be a sign of her mood—many plaits, I decided, meant she was happy. It was her way of singing in silence.

My brothers started leaving the coast when they had earned enough money. Great Bay had become too small. In Sheldon's Bar they drank and smoked and talked about women. They left only when the bar closed. Sometimes they spent the rest of the night under a coconut tree. In the morning, they were gone.

We started seeing foreign fishers. They were from Nicaragua and Honduras. Their hair was black and straight and they spoke Spanish. They came for our fish. There were fights with knives and broken bottles.

It is easy to say now that I thought about manhood, that I wondered what the life of a man should be, but I did not. Manhood was like a squall on the sea; it would come and you would not know its force until you were in it. My father fought with my brothers and the house was noisy with their angry words—Silver's engine was dirty, the gas had not been mixed right, they had gone to the wrong place at the wrong time, no fish could possibly have been located there and then. They came back too early or too late. They wasted their earnings on drink. Their traps were poorly repaired and fish escaped. They were excuses for men. I noticed Robert and Ben were taller than my father. Taller and stronger. I no longer had that sense of peace and plenty in our house.

The rock I lie on is called Portland Rock. Slowly told me about it on Gray Pond beach in his mad way, half in Spanish, half in English. That is where the dolphin catchers go, he said. I did not ask him to name the dolphin catchers because I knew them. Bad things go on there, he said, and I knew it was a warning. Still, I took **Water Bird** *to Pedro and then to Portland Rock. Slowly was right. I know who caused me to be here, but I don't know how.*

13

The boys had no way of telling the time. Lloyd thought of being in jail in a dirty cell through nights of dark, slow hours. He would have no friend beside him. He tried to shake off his thoughts—no, sah, he would not be put in jail, even if they caught him. Nobody would bother with that. Maybe he would get a beating or be made to clean the deck.

The sky was cloudy and Lloyd saw that when the moon rose, it would be hidden behind clouds. The sunset was an orange smear over Hellshire. The strong breeze kept off the worst of the mosquitoes and sandflies. They waited.

Night came. Dwight fell asleep. Lloyd sat up straighter and listened to the noises in the bush. He wished a sea turtle would come up on the beach in front of him. It was early in the nesting season, but not impossible. He wished he would hear the breath of a dolphin cruising the deep water just offshore. These were signs of the sea, signs of life, of hope, because they were animals his grandfather loved. "You know sea turtle eat seaweed, Lloydie? Them is like a lawnmower, keep the seaweed short and strong," Gramps had said, the time when they had seen a single turtle hatchling make its way to sea at Tern Cay, struggling over small heaps of sand and mangrove leaves. Lloyd had wanted to help the baby turtle, but Gramps had said no. The turtle's journey was his journey, it could not be avoided. "I thought them eat jellyfish," Lloyd had said, watching the baby turtle scrabbling through beach vines.

"Different kinda turtle. Green turtle eat seaweed; hawksbill eat jellyfish."

Dwight stirred beside him. It was time to get up. The hours spent sitting needed to be walked out of his muscles. Lloyd wanted to spend as short a time as possible in the water. Although it was August and the night was warm, he knew he would start to shiver in the sea if he were there for long. He was glad he had the ice chest—he could hold on to it and it would bear him up, he would not have to tread water while he waited for Dwight to start yelling. He shook his friend awake and they drank from the spare water bottle. He was hungry again.

It was a short walk to the fishing beach and no one noticed the boys on the poorly lit road. Port Royal was a fishing town of less than two thousand people and at night, the men drank and played dominoes on sidewalks, the women operated the bars and sold fried fish from wooden cases, and Kingston people came to Gloria's to eat. A sound system was being set up at the bar closest to the fishing beach. If the music started up, Lloyd wondered if the sailors would hear Dwight's cries.

The fishing beach was empty; the boats pulled high on the beach and the one light on the dock was broken. They sat on an old utility pole behind a storage shed and Lloyd pulled off his shoes. There was a stinking pile of fish guts off to one side and his stomach clenched. He was used to the smell of fish guts; it was fear making his stomach tighten. He stuffed his shoes in the backpack and pushed his fear down. He tied the ice chest and the backpack to the belt loops in his shorts. The chest was white and easy to see, but it would not be unusual to see any kind of garbage floating on the surface of Kingston Harbour.

"You ready?" he said. Dwight had taken off his shoes and shirt and hidden them behind the pole.

"Yeah man. You awright?"

"Ee-hee."

"I did forget to buy the white rum and drink a little, make the sailors smell it on me."

"Don't really matter," said Lloyd. "Just don't make them hold on to you."

"When you think you come back?"

"Late tomorrow."

"Check me, awright?"

"Yeah man, no must?"

They went into the warm, dirty seawater together.

When I was seventeen, Jasmine was my girlfriend. We walked along the stony lanes of Treasure Beach together under the lignum vitae trees and looked for a private place where we could sit and hold hands and maybe kiss. We found a cave on the ridge behind Billy's Bay, a strange place with sand on the floor and big boulders with funny raised round marks. Jasmine said it was an old Arawak cave. The elders said the Arawaks had a line of shelter caves along this ridge until a massive wave came and mashed up their caves and killed them all. She said the big wave brought the huge sand dunes of Treasure Beach and that was how Sandy Bank primary school got its name.

In the cave with Jasmine, I thought of Hatuey, my Arawak prince—I had not thought of him for a long time. But I laughed off Jasmine's story of the massive wave. I brought old feed sacks from Maas Donald, who kept chickens, and lined the floor of the cave. Jasmine and I would sit in the entrance, catching the sea breezes, looking out to the horizon. I was struck by the softness of her palms compared to mine. It was not long before I persuaded her to lie on the floor of the cave with me. Do you think the Arawaks made those marks, she said, pointing to the round things on the boulders. Probably, I said, although they looked more like the kind of tiny plants that grew on rocks in the sea.

Jasmine did not like the sea. It was dangerous, she said. She hated the never-ending noise it made. She wanted to go to Kingston and as soon as she was old enough she would be gone. She did not care if she never saw Great Bay or Billy's Bay or Frenchman's or Calabash Bay ever again. Her mother had taken her to Kingston once and she was full of stories about how it looked—the many cars, the concrete buildings—and the movie theaters. As she chatted, I felt only her hand in mine.

14

The boys paddled along the dark coast. Their feet scraped against hidden things, making them jump. They felt life under the water—long strands of seaweed, small fish. It was an easy swim because behind the solid barrier of the Palisadoes strip, the Harbour was calm. Soon they saw the *Surrey* at anchor, the stern tied to the dock, no more than ten yards from shore. They paused at the old dock that had been covered with birds in the day. It was the last point of good cover.

"You think them finish load already?" Dwight whispered.

"Shh! Make us just look."

The boys huddled behind the low dock. The deck of the *Surrey* was lit and they could see sailors going about their business, coiling ropes, carrying duffel bags and carton boxes. Lloyd was suddenly sure they were about to bring up the forward anchor and loose the stern line. "Me gone," he said. "Wait until you don't see me, then make up plenty noise."

"Awright."

Lloyd sank into the water and began his swim. He let out the twine so the chest floated far behind him. He hated to put his head underwater, but he sank up to his eyes, coming up to breathe. He tried not to make too many ripples. He crossed to the bow of the *Surrey* and then he was in shadow. He breathed more easily. No one would see him here, unless they were looking for him. He rested for a minute at the prow of the ship, feeling the crusted barnacles on the hull below the water line, gathering his strength. The anchor rope was just ahead. He pulled the ice chest closer to him and wrapped the twine several times round his wrist. He waited. He thought of the big propellers under the ship. If they start up the engine now and I fall into the water, me dead, cut up for shark food, he thought. Now, Dwight. Now.

"What the . . . " a sailor said on deck, right over his head. And Lloyd heard the muffled, scratchy sounds of beatbox, Dwight's specialty, and he smiled into the dark. He heard footsteps above him and he imagined the sailors running to the dock side of the *Surrey* and he heard the shouts of the sailors as Dwight moved into his helicopter imitation. It was now or never.

He found the anchor rope with his toes. The sea gave him up with a small struggle. Hand over hand he climbed; there was no give in the anchor rope; the *Surrey* must be tied fast to the dock. The rope scraped the thin flesh behind his knees. Then he was at the deck and he swung himself around to face the ship. He hung from his fingers and for a few seconds he was sure he could not hold on and he would fall into the sea. He tightened his grip on the anchor rope and, kicking to give himself momentum, he hauled himself onto the deck, his chest heaving. He lay still, head down, hoping he looked like a sack or a coiled rope, if anyone looked his way. The air was cold on his skin.

No shouts came in his direction. Dwight's beatbox performance continued and Lloyd raised his head. No one was on deck and the forward hatch was open. He reeled in the twine to bring his chest up. The ice chest tilted to one side and he saw the backpack was going to fall out. He pulled it up quickly; it was heavy and he thought maybe the twine would break. He could see the backpack sliding loose, and he leaned over the edge of the deck as far as he could and grabbed the bag's handle, just as the chest fell away. He cut the twine with his pocket knife and the chest drifted off, bumping along the side of the ship.

He threw his backpack down the hatch and peered into the anchor hold. A dim light glowed on the bulkhead below and he saw at once his stowaway plan was impossible—the deck of the hold was far beneath him, at least six feet down, and the only access was the hatch on the deck. There was no way to get to the rest of the ship. Once the anchor came up, the crew would lock the forward hatch down tight, and he would be trapped without air, covered by the anchor rope and chain, which would fall on top of him in huge heavy coils. He might even be crushed. There was no option—he had to try for the stern.

He tiptoed along the narrow ledge of the *Surrey*'s starboard gunwales toward the stern, hidden behind the main cabin for half the ship's length. He peered around the edge of the cabin—the rest of his journey to the stern would be in plain view. He saw the sailors gathered on the dock, making a circle around Dwight. Some had their backs turned to the ship, but others faced the *Surrey* and no matter how entertained they were by Dwight's diversion they would certainly see him as he ran to the stern. Where would he hide? Then he saw a large inflatable dinghy stored on the deck right up against the transom and there was a small space under its bow.

He looked over at Dwight, still performing, and his friend got louder. The sailors laughed and then Dwight ducked through the circle of men, faking his moves as if playing a game of basketball, and ran for the end of the dock. The men shouted and followed. Lloyd saw his chance and raced for the dinghy. He jumped into the cavity that held the dinghy and slid into the space underneath it.

It was bigger than it looked, but the deck was hard steel and he knew he would be slammed against it by the sea. There was nothing to cushion his passage, no ropes, no stores, just the hull of the dinghy above his head and the deck below. He heard a splash and the men's shouts grew louder. He hoped Dwight had escaped.

Lloyd heard the crew of the *Surrey* returning. They were laughing. "Fool-fool yout'," someone said.

"Ganja mad him," said another sailor. At least the men did not seem angry. The deck quieted down. Minutes passed, and no one shouted at him. He had done it; he really was a stowaway on a Coast Guard ship, bound for the Pedro Bank. Adrenaline had banished his hunger, but he was already thirsty. He let his muscles relax. At least he was on deck, not confined in some airless hiding place below decks where he would have been seasick. He closed his eyes.

He started when he felt the throb of the engines below. He was cramped and cold, but he had dozed. He wondered how long it would take for the *Surrey* to reach the point of no return—that point when even if he were found the ship would continue on its way to Pedro. At least two hours, he figured, maybe three.

What would happen if they found him? Could it happen that he would make it to the Cays and not be allowed off the boat, not be able to talk to anyone? Maybe, if he was found, the captain would have a kind heart, but he knew it was not likely—he had not met many kind men. He listened to the footsteps and voices of the men of the sea around him and hoped they would understand why he was there, hidden under the dinghy.

Then he felt the stern of the *Surrey* swing free, and he heard the sound of ropes being coiled on deck just a few feet from where he lay, the whine of the anchor winch started, the sailors shouted commands, and the boat moved forward. They were finally free of the land. Lloyd allowed his spirits to lift a little. He said good-bye to Dwight in his mind. He hoped he was not at the Port Royal police station, or in some lockup on the Coast Guard base.

A day came when Luke went to Pedro and did not return. He had made the journey with a young fisher called Donovan, who was said to be involved in drugs. Donovan was from Black River; he flashed money around and he owned two fishing canoes. He asked Luke to crew for him although Luke was the more experienced seaman and by rights should have been captain. He offered more money than was customary and Luke went.

They left with another fisher, old Percy in his boat **Lady Joan**. Six days later Percy returned to Great Bay. He hauled up his boat, stored his engine, sold his fish, and later that day showed up at Sheldon's Bar. That is when he asked for Luke and Donovan. The fishers in the bar shook their heads, no, they had not seen the two men. Old Percy said that was strange because they had left Top Cay before him.

Luke and Donovan had gone to drift.

15

The *Surrey* left Kingston Harbour; Lloyd thought it was just after midnight. He knew the instant they rounded the point by the change in the sea under him. He explored his hiding place with his fingers; it was shaped like a triangle with a short base and most of the space was at the apex. He thought he would be most comfortable if he folded himself into the apex, like a half-closed ratchet knife.

He looked around for something to hold on to and, in the murky light, saw there were ropes around the hull of the dinghy. He took hold of one of the ropes and gasped as the first burst of spray hit the deck and found him where he lay. He could hear the chatter of a radio from the flying bridge above his head. He did not know what the men on the bridge could see of the dinghy where he hid, but he hoped they would keep looking ahead.

It was not long before the ship met heavy weather. Up and down the *Surrey* crashed, rocking from side to side as well, the worst of all movements for a boy hidden in a small space. Waves poured over the ship from bow to stern and ran along his body. Lloyd vomited helplessly onto the deck, grateful as each wave washed the vomit away. At least the engine noise was loud. Then Lloyd heard retching sounds nearby. First-time sailor, he thought, and he was glad someone else was being sick. His hiding place seemed to grow smaller and he wished he could walk the deck. Despite his sickness, it would be exciting to be at sea at night in this huge ship, to go farther out to sea than he had ever been.

He had no sense of speed; the *Surrey* seemed to wallow and lurch, but not to move forward. That was one thing about a canoe, even those with small horsepower engines, they raced over the water, fast and nimble, belonging to the sea, at home in it as much as any sea creature. This big ship pounded and churned and fought the sea; it was an invention of man, a machine, and Lloyd thought it would take days to get to the Pedro Cays.

He was cold to his bones and his eyes and lips burned from the spray. The sea was a hard place, a dangerous place, but a man did not complain, he told himself. A man held strong. He tightened his grip on the dinghy ropes and gave himself to the journey. He was going to the place where his grandfather was last seen, and he felt closer to him than at any time since he had disappeared.

The news about Luke traveled around Treasure Beach like the crack of a whip. I was helping Maas Allan mend his pots at the time, near to the buttonwood tree at the end of Calabash Bay. Maas Jacob came running up to me—you no hear, he said? Luke gone to drift. Go tell you mama.

Me? I said. Where Dada is?

Him gone to Black River. Him don't know yet.

I remember the next half an hour because the loss of my brother was both true and not true. It could remain a rumor until I told my mother. Once she knew, it would be so. Where were my elder brothers? This should be their task. For so long elder had meant benefits. But I did not know where they were. At sea, Maas Jacob said vaguely.

Why you think Luke gone to drift? I asked Maas Jacob.

Old Percy did see them leave Top Cay, Maas Jacob said. Old Percy come back.

Mebbe they go Shannon Reef, I said.

Maas Jacob shrugged. Mebbe.

Maas Jacob left me and I sat on the knotted trunk of the buttonwood tree. I was not yet afraid. The words of my Christian schooling came to my mind—let this cup pass from me. I had never understood the imagery—for me, a cup held good things, fish tea and cocoa tea and mint tea. For as long as I sat on the trunk of the buttonwood tree and stared out to sea, my brother would come home.

16

Lloyd realized he could see the rough gray skin of the underside of the dinghy. Dawn was coming. Somehow the night of spray and pounding sea had passed and there was no way he could now be returned to Port Royal before they reached the Pedro Cays. Maybe the shallower water of the Pedro Bank would soon appear? He wanted to see it. His head pounded and his muscles cramped—he had to stand up. He was thirsty enough to lick the deck, but Gramps had drilled it into him: never ever drink seawater, Lloydie. He had stopped vomiting sometime in the night and his body wanted food and water.

Sunlight warmed the deck. Lloyd heard doors opening, the sound of feet on ladders and he smelled coffee. His mouth watered. It was morning and the sea was calming and he could not stand his hiding place a minute more. He slid out from under the dinghy and tried to stand, but his legs buckled. The light of the sun was dazzling. He lay where he had fallen, in plain sight, eyes closed, soaked, shivering, bruised and bloody from the slamming his small body had suffered. He waited to be discovered.

It did not take long. He heard someone say, "But see here now? CAPTAIN!" He opened his eyes and saw two sailors standing over him, wearing blue uniforms and orange life jackets. One held a steaming mug in his hand and Lloyd stared at it. "Captain Blake!" the shorter of the two shouted again. The taller sailor grabbed his arm and pulled him up. "How the hell you get here, bwoy?" Lloyd looked down and said nothing. He would explain himself to the captain.

Soon he was surrounded by a group of sailors, all speaking at the same time. Him look terrible, eeh? Him is a Haitian? Get him some water. Where him was hidin? Anybody know where him come from? Him say anything? Bwoy! What is your name? Mebbe him don't speak English. You in big-big trouble, bwoy! Lloyd's fear was gone; he had stowed away on a Coast Guard boat and what happened next was up to the captain. "Water," he whispered to the man who held him. "Please, sah, me could have some water?"

An older man pushed his way through the sailors. "Sah!" they said and stepped back. "We found this boy on deck," said the tall man. "A stowaway, Captain."

"Have you searched him, McKenzie?" snapped the Captain. He did not sound kind. McKenzie patted Lloyd down and found his pocket knife. "This is all he has, Captain." He held the knife out to the captain, who took it.

"Has he said anything?"

"Him just ask for water, sah."

"Get him some water. And a blanket. Clean him up and take him to my cabin. Get Miller to check him out there. Then bring him to the control room."

"Aye aye, sir."

The sailor called McKenzie hustled him through a hatch inside the ship. Lloyd gasped when he felt the freezing air—the ship was air conditioned. His shivering became uncontrollable. They were in a brightly lit passage with closed doors on either side and the ship still heaved. Lloyd felt sick. McKenzie pushed him along until they came to an open area with a table and a bank of seating. Another sailor brought a folded blanket and held it out to him. Lloyd was shivering so hard he dropped it. McKenzie grabbed the blanket, shook it out, and roughly draped it over his shoulders. It was heavy and Lloyd staggered. His head swam. "Please, sah," he said again, "some water?" He fell to his knees, hunched over, dry retching.

"Him going mess up the place," said the other sailor.

"Bring a bucket," barked McKenzie. "And some water. Never seen anything like this yet."

That day I sat on the buttonwood tree too long and Miss Adina told my mother that Luke was missing. When I walked up to our front door I heard her wailing. She sat with her apron over her head and Miss Adina tried to embrace her, but my mother avoided her offered comfort. Miss Adina counseled prayer. Pastor Peter would call a special service. She looked up and saw me. Conrad, she said. Go find your father. My mother did not lift her head. I turned and went outside to where Maas Lenny and his taxi waited for passengers.

During the drive to Black River I thought about my brothers. Which one of us was my mother's favorite? If she had to pick the one to lose, who would she sacrifice? I was sure it would be me, the last one, the smallest one, the one measuring the least investment of time.

The road to Black River was just a track back then, with a few marled areas where there were cattle farms and giant guango trees. We raised a thin dust as we drove and I remember the dry heat and the tinny sound from Maas Lenny's radio. He spoke only once at the beginning of the journey, to tell me Luke would be fine, he would come home, God always answered prayers if they were made with a clean heart. I knew this was not true.

We drove over the bridge and into Black River. I had not the first idea how to go about finding my father but I was glad to have something to do. We try the market first, Maas Lenny said.

A fisher on the river bank told us my father was up the river trapping shrimp. I had never eaten a shrimp and did not know my father knew how to catch them. While Lenny talked to the fisher, I sat on an old dock and stared at the calm, wide river. This close to the sea, it was one great moving body of water. I watched the birds in the mangroves and the fallen leaves floating by. It was only the second time I had been to Black River and I had never been on its waters. I knew crocodiles lived in the river. I got up and went over to Maas Lenny. He was trying to persuade the fisher to go up the Black River to get my father. Is his son, man, Maas Lenny said. Is an emergency. Life and death, man.

The fisher sighed. Me soon come, he said, and he walked away without urgency. I was sure he would not return and I wanted to hit him, or at least to steal his boat, which sat right there, moored to the dock, engine at the ready. Just cool, Maas Lenny said. The sun had passed its high point and soon it would be afternoon and once night fell we could no longer tell ourselves that Luke and Donovan had simply made a stop at Shannon Reef.

The fisher came back with a woman carrying a basket, and she took his fish and walked away. Make us go then, he said.

We got into his canoe.

17

"I'm the ship's medic," said Miller. He took Lloyd into a tiny cabin, peered into his eyes and mouth, took his temperature, and made him drink from a bottle of water in small sips. He was matter of fact but not rough. He listened to his chest with an instrument. "When last you eat, bwoy?" he said.

Lloyd had to think for a moment. He felt he had been on the *Surrey* for days. "Yesterday, sah. Me brought some bulla in my bag, but me lost it. Aaah!" he cried out, as Miller swabbed his cuts and bruises with something cold and stinging.

"We don't have clothes your size, but put on this T-shirt anyway," he said. "You can eat a bully beef sandwich? A cup of mint tea?"

"Thank you, sah. Thank you."

"Don't thank me, bwoy. You in more trouble than you been in

your life. You stowaway on a Coast Guard boat; you really lick you head!"

Lloyd dried with the rough blanket and stripped off his shirt. He wished he had dry shorts—maybe McKenzie could retrieve his bag. He realized it must be buried under a pile of soaking anchor rope. The medic opened the door and called for the sandwich and the tea. Lloyd was becoming used to the motion of the ship. He looked around him, the gray steel hull, the bed with tightly stretched sheets, the small desk with a laptop computer open, a narrow cupboard door. He wondered if they were below the surface of the sea and wished the medic's cabin had a porthole. "Sit," he said to Lloyd. "Not on the bed! Take my chair."

There was a knock on the door and Miller opened it. A sailor handed him a plate with a sandwich on it and a mug. Lloyd could smell the mint in the tea and he grabbed for the mug. The tea was almost boiling and burned his lips, but oh it was delicious. Gramps loved mint tea; he gave it to Lloyd whenever he was sick. The aromatic tea warmed him from the inside. He ate the sandwich in three bites—the hard dough bread was cut thick and the chunks of bully beef were salty and filling. The medic watched him. "Come," he said, when Lloyd had drained the last drop of tea and wiped his hands on his wet shorts. "Time to see the captain. What you name?"

"Lloyd. Lloyd Saunders, sah."

"Drink some more water and we go."

Lloyd took his time drinking the water. It was too cold in the belly of the ship and the air had a strange dry metallic smell. He didn't want to talk to the captain. He looked around the small cabin, with its cupboards and bunk. The ship seemed like a strange house to him, a house that went to sea, but a house with electricity and running water and bedrooms and a kitchen where mint tea could be made. There were probably even bathrooms—Lloyd realized he needed one. "Sah, could . . . could I use the toilet first?"

"The head?" said Miller. Lloyd wasn't sure what he meant, but he nodded. They came out of the cabin and the medic knocked on another closed door. He opened it and Lloyd saw a closet-like space with a toilet. "See that handle at the side?" said the medic. "Crank it up and down when you done."

There was a tiny basin next to the toilet and Lloyd turned on the faucet. Whoy, he said softly when fresh water came out of the tap. There was no towel on which to dry his hands and face—the sailors probably brought their own kit into the bathroom—the *head*, he corrected himself. He knew there were special names for things on boats. He would learn them. He wondered if he could become a sailor on a Coast Guard boat. He would want to be a sailor on the bridge, in the control room, though, not one below in a cabin. He hoped they would let him climb the ladder to the bridge so he could see what the ocean looked like from way up high.

I remember marveling at the calmness of the river, the way the prow of the boat cut through the water and how the wake seemed oiled. The mangrove trees towered over the river and the down-growing roots were as thick as a man's arm. The river forked and the fisher—Maas Len, he told us—took the western fork and then the river took a wide curve through logwood and guango trees and banks of wild cane and other plants I had not seen before. We turned into a tributary—Slipe River, Maas Len said—and the wide river became smaller and Maas Len cut the engine and we glided. There was no shade and despite the coolness of the water under the canoe, the heat was fearsome.

The tributary became so narrow that vegetation brushed at the side of the boat and Maas Len pulled the engine over the stern, and picked up a long stick. He poled the boat along, leaning heavily on the stick, finding a rhythm born of long practice. The river was now more land than sea and the vegetation on the banks was tall. Mosquitoes swarmed. I had never been anywhere on land so silent.

The river came to a circular pool, where it seemed to end. The plants crowded in. And there a few boats were moored, and in one of them, my father was loading his boat with cone-shaped baskets. He looked up and saw me, and said only these words: Which one? Which one of my sons has gone to drift?

18

"Come in," Captain Blake said. Miller took Lloyd's arm and they went inside, the boy almost tripping over the blanket that was still draped around his shoulders. The control room was full of dials and equipment. "Sir!" said Miller, coming to attention. "The stowaway. Lloyd Saunders. He's a little dehydrated, some cuts and bruises, but no infectious diseases as far as I can see. No fever. Lungs clear."

"Thank you, Lieutenant. Did he have something to eat?"

"Bully beef sandwich, sir. Polished it off. And some mint tea."

"Dismissed."

"Sir!" Miller left the control room and shut the door behind him.

"You're in deep trouble, youngster," said the captain. His voice was rough but he did not sound cruel.

Lloyd met his eyes. "Me know, sah. My granddaddy is lost at sea. Him been missin almost a week. The last place him go is Pedro. Me had to come look for him."

"You could have just asked the Coast Guard to look for him."

"Me do that—we do that. But them not so interested in one old fisher."

This was the wrong thing to say. The captain was not pleased. "The Coast Guard will search for any lost Jamaican."

"Yes, sah, but me is his grandson, and . . . "

"Lloyd Saunders? Is that right? How old are you?" The captain picked up a pen and began to write on a large yellow pad.

"Soon be thirteen," said Lloyd, although his birthday was months away.

"Do your parents know where you are?"

"Told my mother me was crewing for a fisher; no, she don't know."

"And your father?"

"Him don't know."

"How did you get on board the *Surrey*?"

Lloyd told his story. He left out Dwight's part in his daring plan—he did not want to tell the captain his friend's name. He could see the captain did not believe him, but he did not ask him for more details about the beatbox artist. He told the captain of his first visit to the base with Jules—he hoped the captain knew who she was. It was good to have high-up friends. The captain wrote on his pad, stopping him every now and then to ask a question. Lloyd realized the sea was much calmer and his eyelids felt heavy. He thought he could sleep for days. He thought of his dry, steady bed at home with longing.

An intercom squawked. "Arriving at Middle Cay, sir," said a hollow voice.

"Thank you." Captain Blake stood. "Well, you went through a lot to get here, youngster. I'll say that for you. Leave me now. I will deal with you later. Foster! Take him below. Stay with him."

"Please, Captain, let me stay on deck. Me don't . . . me want to see."

The captain looked at him. "Underneath the dinghy, eh? Foster, he can stay on deck but don't let him out of your sight. After we anchor, I'll decide what to do with him."

"Aye aye, sah!" Foster said and saluted.

They went onto the deck and into bright sunshine. Lloyd squinted. Sailors stood around the ship at their posts and the *Surrey*'s engines raced. He sat on one edge of the dinghy he had hidden under while the *Surrey* made several attempts to anchor, the engines racing, sailors shouting orders. Lloyd heard the rattle of the anchor chain and wondered if he would be able to get his bag. Finally, the sailor on the forward deck shouted that the anchor held and the engines shut down. For a moment, there was silence and an air of relief on the *Surrey*. Then the voices of the sailors started as they made ready to disembark. Lloyd could see Middle Cay in the distance—probably the water was too shallow for the big ship to anchor closer to the cay.

The sailors gathered on the stern deck. They carried duffel bags and their faces were glum—it did not seem they wanted to spend a week on Middle Cay, exchanging places with the previous week's shift. Lloyd wondered where on the Cay they stayed after the *Surrey* left them. Wherever it was, he was sure there would be no fresh water from a tap.

He saw two fishing canoes heading their way, leaping over the waves. One of the canoes came alongside where there was a ladder. Sailors jumped into the canoe. Orders were shouted, lines were cast and caught. Lloyd saw it was a tricky operation—the two boats, one large, one small, rode the waves at different rates and waves pushed and pulled the canoe against the hull of the *Surrey*, the gap widening and closing. The sailors made a line and began passing stores and bags down to the canoe. They worked quickly and the air was filled with curses.

Lloyd had to leave the *Surrey*. Foster was nearby but watching the activity on deck. Could he simply jump onto the next canoe? The sun beat down and even so early in the morning, he began to sweat. The heat was good—he had been cold for so many hours. He loved the smell of the sea breeze and he felt he was in a place he knew well, in the open air on a boat that rode the waves. He was still thirsty. He needed his bag.

He left his place on the dinghy and headed to the gunwale. "Don't even think about it, bwoy," said the captain.

Lloyd turned and saw him descending the ladder from the bridge.

"Me was just going to look for my bag," he said.

"Where you left it?"

"Me threw it down where the anchor rope go. Me was going to hide in there, but it too deep."

"My God. You would have died in there." Captain Blake shook his head. "Okay. Follow me. Foster!" They went to the bow of the *Surrey*. Two sailors stood on deck and saluted as the captain walked onto the forward deck. Lloyd saw the hatch was open.

"This boy's bag is in the anchor well," Captain Blake said. "Any chance you could get it out, Foster?"

"Aye aye, sah!" Foster eased himself into the hatchway—it was a tight fit. One of the other sailors peered into the well. "See it there!" he said. "In a plastic bag. No, the other side."

Foster handed the bag to the other sailor and climbed out of the anchor hold. The few moments he had spent in confinement below had beaded his forehead with sweat. Lloyd shivered. He could have died there. Captain Blake handed the bag to him. It was squashed, but intact and fairly dry. Lloyd sat on the deck and searched inside for the bullas. He found them in their wrapping, reduced to crumbs. He pulled out the water bottle and took a long drink. It made him thirstier. His spare clothes in the bag were dry. "Can I change, sah?" he said to Captain Blake.

"Take him below, Foster," said the captain. "Don't let him out of your sight."

That first night when we all knew Luke had gone to drift we ate boiled pepper shrimp with our fingers. My father's shrimp, my mother's cook pot. She spread newspaper over the kitchen table and the seven of us huddled around it—a table that once held us all easily as boys was now too crowded. No one spoke. We shelled the shrimp with tiny ticking sounds. The pepper they had been cooked in burned our fingers, but our mother did not warn us about touching our eyes. The food stuck in our throats, but our mother said it was not to be wasted. I have never been able to stand the taste of shrimp since.

We began our wait. At first, it was all of Great Bay that waited, in groups of men and women, gathered on the beach, in bars and cook sheds and grocery shops and under trees. Then the waiting spread to other fishing villages—to Calabash Bay and Billy's Bay and Frenchman's. The men talked in low voices about where Donovan and Luke could have gone. Everyone agreed the weather was fair and the problem must be engine trouble. The women hardly spoke. When night fell, kerosene lamps were lit and those who had electricity turned it on. As the moon rose, the groups of people thinned but never completely disappeared. The Treasure Beach communities always kept their vigil for anyone gone to drift.

I stayed with my father at Sheldon's Bar. He hardly seemed to notice my presence. He had told my brothers that when the light of day came we would all go to sea to look for Luke. No one would go alone—we would travel in pairs and we would stay in plain sight of one another. I did not say anything, but I thought this to be a poor plan for finding a small canoe, lost at sea.

19

Lloyd sat on the stern of the *Surrey*, legs overboard, staring at Middle Cay. He had eaten all the bulla crumbs and drank half the bottle of water. He had gone to the bathroom—the head—three times. His headache had gone. He was glad to be back in his own clothes. How would he get onto the cay to ask his questions? It was too far to swim. He could not face the thought of coming this far, surviving that pounding night and not being allowed off the ship.

The *Surrey* was quiet except for the noise of the generator. The sun was well up. The captain was on the bridge with one other sailor. Lloyd climbed up the ladder. "Captain," he said.

"What you want, bwoy?"

"Please, sah. Please let me go onto Middle Cay. Please let me talk to the fishers."

Captain Blake made a sound of irritation. Lloyd waited. He looked around, liking the high vantage point. He could see two other islands and many fishing canoes at sea. There was also a big commercial fishing vessel anchored much farther offshore than the *Surrey*. "Conch fishers," said the captain, following his gaze. Lloyd wondered if it would have been better to seek passage with the conch fishers. He had heard they used young boys to dive for the conch, breathing air through a long hose to a machine that sat on the surface of the sea. Perhaps they would have given him a job and he would not have to beg to be allowed on Middle Cay.

"You go to sea with your granddaddy?" said Captain Blake.

"Yes, sah. From me a baby."

"You close to him, then?"

Lloyd knew he did not have the right words for his relationship with Gramps. "Yes, sah," he agreed.

"So tell me what happened to him."

"Nuttn more to tell. Him don't fish at Pedro, but him go last Sunday. Him call us on Tuesday, say he comin back on Thursday. But him don't come back. Him not answerin the phone."

"You talk to fishers at Port Royal and Gray Pond and Rocky Point?"

"Yes, sah. Not Rocky Point. Too far. The fishers at Gray Pond beach say to ask the Coast Guard." Me tell you this already, he wanted to say. He remembered the way Captain Blake had reacted to the suggestion that the Coast Guard would search only for important people.

"Well, youngster, you have guts, I'll say that for you. And it's good you love your granddaddy. Come. I will get you onto Middle Cay and we see what we see. Don't hold out too much hope though. I checked. Commander Peterson did tell the Middle Cay detail to ask around. Your granddaddy was here, but he left on Thursday and nobody out here seen him since."

Lloyd let the words pass over him like the bursting spray on his long journey. "Thank you, sah," was all he said in response. You don't know everything, he thought.

Squall after squall came to Portland Rock last night and I was happy to exchange sleep for water. I stripped off all my clothes and lay naked under the sky on the life jacket. At dawn I was cleansed but when I tried to stand, I fell. In the dark I had not been able to fill the plastic bottle. My right leg aches and aches. The whelks are finished and the gulls are very loud this morning. I imagine they are disappointed I have not yet died. It is good to lie washed under the open sky. I listen for the sound of a boat and I don't know what to hope for because if it is the wrong boat, I am finished.

20

Lloyd and Foster walked the narrow alleys between the dwellings on Middle Cay. Most of the shacks were empty and Lloyd realized this was another obstacle—the fishers were already at sea. Perhaps by the time they returned to the cay the *Surrey* would have weighed anchor and be heading back to Port Royal. Maybe the captain would let him stay on Middle Cay. He could return to the mainland with any fisher. He knew his mother would worry more with each passing night, but he could get a message to her. Maybe the captain himself would call her.

He was surprised to see women on Middle Cay. Two very young women wearing wigs and skimpy clothing sat on an old boat engine outside one of the shacks. A much older woman squatted over a basin, cleaning fish. Fish scales clung to her forearms. Some of the shacks were actually shops with shelves lined with tins of Vienna sausages and bully beef and mackerel, bags of flour, sodas, beer, rum, even clothes. Some shacks contained several rooms, others were just a single room enclosed in plywood and zinc. A man slept in a slung hammock in one of the houses, the door open to catch the sea breeze. Lloyd saw barrels containing water and some shacks had rusty gutters for collecting rainwater.

He saw a generator outside one of the bigger dwellings. There were two small but substantial buildings on the island, one rectangular and the other looking like a huge can, half buried in the sand. The sailors were gathered around the rectangular building—the Middle Cay Coast Guard base, Lloyd figured. The other building was locked. There was a large area of smoking garbage off to one side and seabirds circled in the sky, making their loud calls. A woman walked out of one of the shacks and threw fish guts onto the beach. The birds descended on it, shrieking and pecking.

"Where you want to start, bwoy?" snapped Foster, clearly annoyed by the duty he had been assigned. Lloyd looked around. The women avoided his eyes. They were probably afraid of the sailors and unlikely to talk freely in their presence. "Sah?" he said. "You can wait somewhere for me? Me can't run from the Cay. Them not going talk to me if you standin right there."

Foster kissed his teeth. "Awright, bwoy," he said. "See that building over there? The base. Me wait for you there. One hour. That's it. Then we going back to the *Surrey*. If me have to search for you, me personally lock you in a cabin until we back at Cagway. You get me?"

"Yes, sah."

"And don't go that side." The sailor pointed past the burning garbage to one end of the cay where there were three damaged concrete structures. "Middle Cay bathroom is the beach. Captain, he don't want any mess on the *Surrey*."

Lloyd nodded and set off. Middle Cay was like every fishing beach he had ever visited—old boats pulled up out of the reach of all but the highest seas, piles of nets, fish pots, rusting gear. Strong smells of salt and fish. There were hundreds of birds, including a type he had never seen, pure white with the amber eyes of a goat behind a mask—those birds held the ground near the garbage, despite the heat and smoke.

※ ※ ※

It took him less than an hour to speak to everyone he saw on Middle Cay. One woman with the best stocked shop remembered Maas Conrad. Her name was Miss Alice, and she said she had lived near Gray Pond one time. Yes, Maas Conrad had been at Pedro, he had bought a fried fish from her and a bottle of Stone's Ginger Wine, and they had chatted about the old days when fish were plentiful in Kingston Harbour. "The elders, them always talk about that," she said to Lloyd, although it was clear she was too young to remember those days.

"Was he okay?" said Lloyd. "Not sick or anything?"

"Him not sick. Him soon come back, man."

The few fishers on Middle Cay told the same story. Yes, they had seen Maas Conrad, they knew about his catch, which had been reasonable, they had shared a drink with him, he had watched TV at night over at Miss Leona's bar, until the generator went off, and when they woke on Thursday morning Maas Conrad had gone. They did not know if his phone had stopped working; he had not said so. He had sold some of his catch to the men who plied packer boats back and forth to the mainland. They assumed he had fished early on the morning of his departure and had left for Port Royal or Rocky Point right after. The weather was not the calmest, but there were no storms. Unless his engine had failed, they were all sure he would turn up.

Lloyd had no watch, but he knew his hour was almost up. He was near tears—all for nothing, he thought, all this way for nothing. He walked away from the shacks and onto the beach, looking for a secluded place where he could sit for a minute and stare out to sea. He found a slice of shade beside a wrecked fishing canoe and sat on a rock. The waves came in and out, foaming at his feet.

"But see yah now, is Lloydie! What you doing out here alone?" Lloyd turned to see Slowly, the fisher who had been lost at sea and ate seaweed to survive.

"Wha'ppen, Slowly?" he said. "What you doin out here?"

Lloyd saw the canoe was just a shell and there was some kind of bedding laid out near the bow. Slowly must have been asleep in the canoe, his head under the bow cap for the little shade it offered. Did he now live there, in an old canoe, open to sun and rain? His clothes were rags and his skin was crusted with salt and fish scales and sweat.

His eyes shone with a mad light.

"What me doing out here? Staying close to God, Lloydie. This is where him go come to take us up. Him go come in the night and me is ready. Mine eyes have seen the GLORY of the coming of the LORD . . . " Slowly leapt out of the canoe and, turning in a circle, stretched his arms out. Then he belted out the rest of the hymn, marching in place on the sand. Poor Slowly, Lloyd thought. Him turn madman. It was time to go to the Coast Guard base for the journey back to the mainland. He stood up. "Awright, Slowly. Me gone. You take care."

"Wait!" Slowly said. "Wait wait wait wait wait. *El mal en la tierra*. God has loosed the fateful lightning of his terrible swift sword. Them got him, Lloydie. The foreign man got him. The sins of the father got him, carried down from generation to generation. *El mal en la tierra*. You have drinks money for me? A smalls?" His last request was made in a normal voice.

Lloyd shook his head. "Sorry, man, don't have any money with me."

"Is awright man. Likkle Lloydie. What a way you grow big! You far from home out here. Bwoy, be fearful of the sea, for it contain the leviathan! You hear me, yout'?"

"Me hear you, Slowly. Me gone though." Lloyd turned and walked toward the Coast Guard base. He fought his tears. Behind him he heard Slowly start on another hymn. At the door to the base, Lloyd looked back across the sand. Slowly was playing imaginary drums. Suddenly he stopped. He pointed at Lloyd. And then he began a strange movement with his arms, almost like the shape of waves, a kind of dance. "Watch me, Lloydie!" he shouted from the beach. "Me know the truth! Black Crab know the truth! Find the dolphin catchers. Go talk to Maas Roxton. Find a rock in the sea." He continued his weird dance in the sun.

Lloyd ran back to him. "What you saying, Slowly? Beg you talk sense. Black Crab is a man?"

Slowly widened his eyes and again rattled off a string of Spanish phrases.

"Talk English," Lloyd pleaded, holding Slowly's arm. "And talk slow. Everything is cool, Slowly. Just cool."

"Yout'! Find youself over here!" It was Foster shouting at him from the Coast Guard base. His time on Middle Cay was over. Lloyd tugged at Slowly's arm and held the man's gaze. "Slowly, me is begging you, who is Black Crab and what him have to do with Gramps?"

"Forget Black Crab. The evil thrive like the green bay tree and evil is abroad in the land. Abroad in the land, me say. Talk to him friend, Maas Conrad friend. You know him? Maas Roxton. Him live at Rocky Point. Go to him, Lloydie. Go to him fast-fast."

Lloyd heard steps behind him and Foster grabbed his arm. "Me hear you, Slowly," he said, as Foster dragged him away. "Bless up."

"You waste you time talking to a madman, bwoy," sneered the sailor. "You fool-fool just like him."

At the entrance to the base, Lloyd looked back again. Slowly was still doing his strange dance on the beach. And Lloyd remembered Gramps's dolphin stories and his descriptions of how they moved through the water, up and down at the surface. Slowly's dance was a dolphin dance. Definitely, his grandfather's disappearance had something to do with dolphins. Lloyd felt a bubble of hope in his chest. He knew Maas Roxton, his grandfather's best friend. He should have thought of going to see him first. And he had another name, a name his parents knew—Black Crab.

Lloyd joined the sailors going back to the mainland, anxious for the return journey to be over.

Lewis and I went together to look for Luke. My second oldest brother was twenty by then, a big man. He lived in Junction in the hills with a woman our mother disliked because her hair was not processed and stuck out from her head. Our mother did not think this was decent. I wondered if Lewis missed living close to the sea. As we left the beach in the glow of dawn I hoped he remembered how to navigate. And then I realized that I had learned all there was to learn about being at sea, all that could be taught man to man, and if Lewis lost his way I could take us both home.

But the sea revealed nothing that day, nor the next, nor the day after that. We traveled aimlessly, always in sight of the other canoe with Ben and Robert in it, and I thought we should have a better plan. Our search was limited by fuel but was guided by nothing. My father looked old for the first time.

Those days were cloudless and the sea as unyielding as metal. I thought my eyes would go blind with staring into a hurtful glare, at a sweeping horizon that held nothing at all. We saw other fishing boats at sea, and each time we saw them in the distance, our spirits would lift for a short time and then would sink as we identified the boat and its occupants.

I found myself looking for the dolphins. The sea seemed empty of life; now, I doubt my memory, but I remember no man o'war bird diving from the sky, no leaping ray, no swirl of jack schooling beneath the surface. But the dolphins did not come and I knew the sea was a grave.

Luke went to drift in his boat and now I am lost at sea on a small piece of land, a rock in the sea. My brother must have been certain we, his family, would look for him. I think now about my own eyes and the eyes of my father and my brothers and all the eyes of the Treasure Beach villagers, turned to the sea, searching for Luke, and I wonder whose eyes are looking for me now.

21

All the sailors were on board the *Surrey* getting ready for the journey back to Port Royal and the Cagway base and there was an air of anticipation. Lloyd heard them talking. They longed to be on the mainland, back to city life. Men of the sea they might be but they were not fishers and they were glad their week on a tiny island in the middle of the Caribbean sea was over. The *Surrey*'s engines finally started and the anchor was brought up.

Lloyd realized how weary he was. He was hungry again; and thirsty. He wondered if Captain Blake would let him sleep in one of the bunks. He felt sure he would no longer be seasick below deck. "Move from there, bwoy!" a sailor shouted at him. He got up and stood, facing the setting sun. The wake of the *Surrey* streamed away behind them and Middle Cay grew smaller and smaller until it disappeared.

Captain Blake sent Lloyd into his cabin below. Foster gave him several blankets and Lloyd piled them on the floor. He was drunk with the need to sleep. He had refilled his water bottle and eaten another bully beef sandwich. The *Surrey* wallowed and surged over the waves and Lloyd waited to feel seasick, but his stomach was steady. Foster had given him a bucket and warned him to use it. Lloyd felt proud that the bucket would be empty in the morning. He wedged himself between the captain's desk and the hull and climbed into the nest of blankets. For a moment, he wished for darkness because the lights in the cabin were still on. Then his eyes closed and he was asleep.

"Wake up, bwoy," someone said, shaking his shoulder. Lloyd opened his eyes. Foster stood in the cabin, holding a mug of mint tea. "We almost in," he said. "Time to get up. Here." He handed Lloyd the mug of tea. "You lucky, bwoy. The captain like you. Maybe you don't end up in the lockup, where all like you belong." Lloyd heard footsteps on the deck and the shouts of the sailors—they must be near to Port Royal.

It was still dark outside. Lloyd had wanted to see the sun rise, to take a last look across the sea for Gramps before they entered the familiar waters of the Port Royal Cays and Kingston Harbour, but he sensed

in the calming of the sea that they would soon be at berth. He turned

to face the bow and saw the lights of Kingston. They were very close.

Cagway base was brightly lit and a single sailor stood on the dock

to receive the *Surrey* into port. Lloyd realized no one was watching

him. He took a last drink from the hot tea and poured the rest of it

overboard. He set the mug in the circle made by a coil of rope. As the

gap between the ship and the dock narrowed, Lloyd took his chance.

He jumped onto the dock and ran away into the night. He heard a

sailor call out—"Hey!"—but then he heard the slapping sound of ropes

cast and fallen, curses from the *Surrey* and the engines racing as the

ship docked. He dodged around a small low structure built almost in

the sea and headed for the low dock he remembered. He was unsteady

as he ran—the land seemed to rise and fall—and the wet sand gave way

under his feet.

Behind the dock, he slipped into the sea without hesitation. It was

cold and he gasped. There would be no dry clothes at the end of this

swim, but soon the sun would be up and he would be in Port Royal

and then he would be making his way home to Bournemouth and his mother. She would be angry, but he was ready to face her.

He felt as if he had been at sea for months. His bag weighed him down and his swim was slow. Wednesday morning. His grandfather had been missing for just under a week. He wondered where Dwight was. He hoped he could find him—they would laugh together over his beatbox performance. He walked out of the sea onto the Port Royal fishing beach just as the sun came up.

As the search for Luke went on, the pace of ordinary life in the four fishing villages slowed and almost halted. The talk about what could have happened to Luke and Donovan ended like a dripping standpipe, finally fixed. There was nothing more to be said. The counting of the days stopped too—at first, there was discussion of how long a man could survive at sea without water, without food, and there were stories of men long forgotten, except that they had gone to drift. These two men were fishers, it was pointed out. They had their gear. Luke and Donovan would be able to catch fish and turtles and even seabirds. They would not starve. Then the older fishers would warn about the emptiness of the deep sea, how difficult it was to catch fish when the seafloor was too far beneath the surface.

Everyone knew the limitation was water—that without water there were only a few days of life left to a man trapped in an open canoe. And everyone saw the high white sky over Treasure Beach that held not a single rain cloud. When the fifth day passed, talk about food and water ceased. Slowly the groups of people who waited for the return of my brother and the man called Donovan dispersed, but although it was not easy to see, the villagers still waited behind closed doors.

By the sixth day after Luke went to drift I was tired of the aimless search. I had never found the sea to be a lifeless place, but in the search for my brother it held a blankness that made me want to leave Great Bay. To occupy the blazing hours I thought about what it would be like to live in the middle of the island, perhaps in Mandeville, at the top of a hill with the sea only an idea, a story, a blue blur at the end of vision. Maybe Jasmine would leave with me and we could make our lives in a gentler place of green, a place with cool nights and flowers around a small house. But I could never see what I might do in such a place.

Today is my sixth day on Portland Rock and I am thinking of the sixth day of the search for my brother. I am on a rock, he was in a boat. Water Bird is lost. I am sick of the taste of sea snails and whelks. I want a full bottle of Red Stripe beer or Stone's Ginger Wine. I want a plate full of curry goat and rice. I want the sight of other people, the softness of a bed, the shelter of a roof.

22

Lloyd lay on his bed, alone at home, his arms behind his head. He had dried his clothes on the beach near the fort before returning home. He had washed from the bucket in the yard and eaten half of a stale bun found at the back of the food cupboard. He longed for chicken and rice, maybe even some breadfruit, a big plate of cooked food swimming in gravy. He wished again for a cell phone—he could call Dwight, tell him he was back, boast of his adventures.

His body felt used up as if the sea had sucked something from him. He thought of the black sea eggs pot fishers used as bait, handling them in gloved hands, putting them in the pots along with orange peel and coconut, punching them open with a spear before the pot was lowered into the sea. They had yellow yolks, like the eggs of chickens, which drifted through the water in faint trails, attracting fish to swim into the pot and become trapped there. Gramps said sea eggs were important because they ate the weeds on the reef.

Once, snorkeling on the reef at Lime Cay, Lloyd had seen a starfish chase a sea egg in the slowest of slow motion, eventually crawling over the spines of the sea egg, holding it fast against the floor of the sea to crush and eat it. An egg that moved, an egg that ate, an egg with defenses that could still be beaten. Gramps had told him how the black sea eggs had all died off one time, for reasons no one knew. Lost at sea he might be, but Lloyd was sure his grandfather still lived. The boy closed his eyes and he slept.

He woke when he heard the front door open. His mother was back. "Lloydie?" she called. Her voice was calm. And then he realized the flaw in his story—he had returned from his fictional fishing trip as crew with neither fish nor money. He pretended to be asleep. He sensed his mother standing in the doorway but she did not call his name again. He heard the clanking of pots and the rustling of plastic bags. She had brought home supper. Joy and hunger rose in his chest. He was home, he was out of danger. His mother was a safe harbor; they had been together for a long time, from his birth. She had shared all his hours, all his days and nights, waking and sleeping. She was always home at night. Their house was a steady, safe place, the opposite of being at sea. His mother made it safe for him, safe for them both. He hoped she had brought home chicken and rice. He heard the crackle of something frying and he was starving.

He got up from his bed and put on an old T-shirt. He went into the small living room, filled with the smell of meat cooking, to his mother, her back turned to him, the ties of her apron around her neck and waist, her head lowered to her task. He saw for the first time that the tight curls of hair around her face and neck were gray. Perhaps he owed her the truth.

She turned when she heard him come into the room. "How the catch?" she said. "What you go with that old fool Popeye for? After him don't know nuttn 'bout fishin. Bet you don't bring home not even one so-so grunt."

And Lloyd nodded. The easiest lies were the ones never spoken. He waited for the next question, as to whether gentle Popeye, so named for his height and thinness and his white beard, had paid him, but the question never came. He saw tension in his mother's shoulders as she cooked. It was dark outside—the day of his return had come and gone.

He put their two plastic place mats and their two plates and their two forks on the rickety table and then he sat in silence, waiting for the food his mother cooked to be ready. He would eat, he would sleep for a few more hours, and then he would go back to his place on the wall at the Gray Pond beach and watch for his grandfather.

On the seventh day of the search, I said good-bye to Luke in my mind. Lewis and I were near the place where we had seen the dolphins and as I always did, I looked for them, but they did not come. It was very still—the sea was held suspended without motion. Ahead was the reef where we often set our pots, and not even there could we see the surge or break of waves. Luke is dead, I thought, and it seemed a small thing, no bigger than the death of any fish we threw into the bottom of our canoe. My brother was not exempt from death; nor was I. I wanted to find his body because I would only then be released from this pointless search, this understanding that life itself was indifferent to any particular life. That day, it was my hand on the tiller while Lewis stood in the bow, staring at the unnatural sheen of the sea through east and west, north and south. I turned Silver for home.

Where you going? Lewis said, when he realized what I was doing.

Me done, I said. Done, finish.

He argued, but I did not speak again. When we neared Great Bay I cut the engine, and at the point where I knew the seafloor was sandy and shallow I vaulted into the water and swam away from the canoe, my eyes burning in the salt water.

23

"Where the bwoy is, you wut'less son?" Vernon Saunders yelled. The front door slammed. Lloyd had gone to bed, intending to sleep for a few hours only, but still tired from his trip to Middle Cay he had not woken to go to the seawall. He sat up, wishing his window was bigger and he could escape. His father was drunk, of course.

"Ssst!" his mother hissed. "Stop you noise! You want everybody hear you damn foolishness? What you going on with?"

"Me no care who want listen. Where him is? LLOYD! Find you backside in here!"

Lloyd got out of bed. His father was free with his fists and his belt, but this was nothing remarkable—most of Lloyd's friends were regularly beaten by mothers and fathers and visiting men; there was almost a pride in it, in being able to take it. But there was something more in his father's voice that worried Lloyd. He pulled on his clothes.

The shower curtain was torn aside and his father stood in the doorway. Lloyd was trapped—he should have walked out himself into the outer room, perhaps he would have been able to dodge his father's blows and get through the front door. If Vernon was really drunk, avoiding him would have been easy. But now he filled the doorway and there was no easy escape.

"Where you tell you mother you go Monday night, bwoy?" he shouted, his face close to Lloyd's, his hands balled up into fists.

"What wrong with you, Vern?" his mother said. "Him did a little crewin for Popeye, that's all. Come outside. Leave the bwoy alone."

"That's what you think! Crew for Popeye? Is a damn lie! You know where you good-good son was Monday night? Him was on the Coast Guard boat! Him stowaway on the Coast Guard boat to Pedro. You lucky him not in jail!"

"Lloydie?" his mother said. "Is true?"

How had his father found out? Lloyd wondered. He stared at the floor.

"Lloydie?" his mother said again, her voice sharper now. Lloyd backed away from his father and reached for the dangling switch to the one lightbulb in his room. He turned it on and his father blinked in the sudden light. Lloyd took his chance and squeezed past his father and out of his bedroom. The front door was shut. His mother caught his arm.

"Hear me dyin trial!" his mother said. "You stowaway on the Coast Guard boat? What you do that for?"

"Me went to look for Gramps," he said. And then a righteous anger filled his chest. He dragged his arm away. "Nobody care! You don't care! Gramps lost at sea and nobody lookin for him. So yes, is true; me go on the Coast Guard boat. And me talk to the fishers on Pedro, but nobody tell me nuttn. Until me see Slowly. Him tell me Gramps have sumpn to do with them foreign people what catch dolphins. Me hear you talkin about it at nighttime. You think me is a fool? Me think Gramps is dead over some foolishness to do with dolphins!"

The loss and fear Lloyd had carried for a week broke like a wave on the sharpest of reefs and he began to cry. He was a twelve-year-old boy. He was not a man. The person he loved most in the world was lost at sea. The days had surged past and with each dawn the chances of finding Gramps alive grew smaller.

"Slowly?" sneered his father. "Bare foolishness! That man don't even have half a mind." He staggered a little.

Lloyd wiped his eyes. It was hopeless. He would never know his grandfather's fate. Perhaps one day the wreckage of his boat would be found, maybe a splintered plank of wood with *Water Bird* written on it would wash up on the coast. *He would never know.* There would never be a grave anywhere, perhaps not even a funeral or a nine night. Maybe he would live the rest of his life waiting for *Water Bird* to round the point at Palisadoes until the span of a human life was finally over. How long would wondering last, how slowly could hope die?

"How old Gramps is?" Lloyd said to his silent parents. They stood apart from each other, but there was something united in the way they looked at him.

"How old you father is?" his mother said to his father, and there was relief in her voice. This was a question they could answer.

"The old fool? Must be sixty-seven, sixty-eight by now."

Lloyd thought of Pastor Errol's sermons about the three score and ten years of life a person was given, according to the Bible, but he knew many people who lived into their eighties and nineties. Even many fishers—despite the life of sun and sea and hardship, they lived and worked until they were very old and sometimes their bodies outlived their minds, and they became like Slowly, talking and dancing to no one. It would be at least twenty years before he could be sure Gramps was not on an island somewhere, not on a lonely beach, not run off with a woman, not migrated to do farm work. Twenty years before Lloyd would know for sure Gramps was dead.

The anger had left the room. Vernon staggered and the smell of rum rolled off him. Lloyd wished his mother would put her arms around him but she was not that kind of woman. He thought then of Jules and the way she had whispered to the Lime Cay dolphin and the story that it had been put on an airplane and taken to another island. He thought of mad Slowly and his dolphin dance. No. He would not give up. Gramps had seen something he should not have seen and someone knew what had happened to him.

"Who is Black Crab?" he said to his mother.

She grabbed his arm again and her nails bit into his skin. "Now you listen me, pickney," she hissed. "You forget you ever hear that name, you hear me? Some things not good to talk. Pickney must *stay outta* big people business!"

"Tell me what happen to Gramps," he pleaded.

"Nuttn don't happen to him," shouted his father. "You hear me? NUTTN!"

The day after I abandoned the search for my brother I climbed the limestone rocks behind the villages alone. The weather was turning—there was a low bank of cloud at the horizon and as I watched, the cloud changed from the white of wood smoke to the purple of a storm. It was too late for Luke. I had not gone home the night before because I did not want to see my mother or father. I had found the long abandoned hull of Birdie, covered in a tangle of beach rose vines and bird droppings, and I had crawled inside.

In the morning, my mouth was foul and my stomach empty. I had no water. This was how Luke would have felt on that first day when he first confronted the dead engine or the loss of the expected sight of land, before he knew his life was almost over. What would it be like to count the time you had left with certainty, to know however bad you felt on the first morning, you would only feel worse on the next and worse still on the day after that? To try to hold on to hope, to let yourself feel it in tiny amounts, like scarce sips of water? My brother was dead at seventeen and rage made me short of breath. Rage at our father for taking us to sea; at Donovan—it must have been his fault because the Saunders men had always been safe at sea; at God himself for not raising his all-powerful hand to save my brother; at myself for failing to find him, for losing hope and turning away.

From my vantage point, I could see the tiny shapes of fishing canoes going out and coming in and the sea began to curl and surge. Soon there were whitecaps and the cloud at the horizon spread and grew and became heavy with rain. My stomach cramped. The limestone rocks were sharp. I thought of Jasmine sitting beside me in the Arawak cave and she seemed like someone I had known too long ago to matter. The first drops of rain fell.

Soon a solid curtain of rain obscured the coast. I stripped off my shorts and undershirt and stood in the downpour. I turned my face to the sky and opened my mouth and I drank, and my stomach churned and knotted. The rain squall was heavy and short and when it was *over I pulled on my wet, filthy fishing clothes and climbed down the hill toward Great Bay. I turned onto the track that led down to Great Bay, and then I saw a crowd on the beach and I heard raised voices. Perhaps someone had landed a shark. I did not hurry. There was nothing on that beach to make me quicken my step. Then Maas Lenny ran past me and I heard Maas Jacob shout to him, them is really back? The crowd parted as I came near and I saw Silver drawn up on the sand, and I saw my father standing next to my mother who held my brother in her arms.*

I ran to them. Luke? I said and my voice broke. I saw my mother supporting my brother; it did not seem he could stand on his own. She fed him sips of water from a cup. His eyes were closed and he did not seem to hear me. He was bird-like, skin over bones. I saw my brothers standing nearby with lowered heads. We were silent and my heart pounded as if I faced a mortal enemy. The crowd around us was jubilant and the women praised the good Lord and his son Jesus Christ and arms were lifted to the sky. People asked questions of Luke and of each other—When him reach? Who find him? What did happen? The engine fail? Other voices made their contributions—me never did trust that Donovan. You see the power of prayer?

Donovan. I looked around. Only one man had come home.

24

The security guard at Morgan's Harbour Hotel greeted Lloyd as if they were friends. "Wha'ppen, yout'?" he said. "You come back? What you name again? For the book."

Lloyd told him his name. He had found Jules's business card, borrowed Maas Benjy's cell phone, and called her. She sounded as if she had been doing something important, but she agreed to meet him.

He walked into the hotel. Jules was sitting on a low couch across from the front desk with another woman, blond haired and freckled, clearly a foreigner. The two women got up as he walked up to them and Jules held out her hand. "Lloyd," she said. "You granddaddy come back yet?"

"No, Miss," he said, shaking her hand, liking the way she treated him as an equal, a big person.

"You don't hear anything from Commander Peterson?"

"No. But I did go to Pedro," he said in a rush. "I hid on *Surrey*."

"You did *what*?" she said.

"I did stowaway. And a man on Middle Cay tell me Gramps get involve with catchin dolphins and I want you to tell me about it."

Jules shook her head. "You were a stowaway on a Coast Guard boat! And they didn't lock you up?"

"No, Miss. Tell me about the dolphin business."

"Where to start?" she said, more to herself than to him. She gestured toward the white woman. "Lloyd, this is Madison Barry. She's from the US. She studies dolphins too, but mostly the ones that have been captured."

The American woman held out her hand too and Lloyd shook it. She was very thin and her hair was chin length and straight, bleached by the sun. Her eyes were blue, and the skin was crinkled at the corners. Lloyd thought she looked older than she was. Too much sun, probably. She smiled and her teeth were white and straight. "Very glad to meet you, Lloyd," she said.

"Let's sit down," Jules said. She led the way onto the dock. Lloyd saw that the big white boat he had noticed last time was gone but the bartender was the same man. Jules ordered and paid for drinks and they sat at the table farthest away from the bar.

"So. The dolphin trade," Jules said. "Basically, there are people—traders—who catch dolphins from the wild and sell them to tourist attractions in lots of different countries. Madison and I are trying to stop this trade—many people are working to stop it."

"Why?" Lloyd said.

"Why what?"

"Why you tryin to stop it?" He thought dolphins should be left in the sea where they belonged; after all, they were not eaten and he knew Gramps would not approve of the captures, but if the tourist places needed dolphins, they had to come from somewhere. And if money was to be made from capturing dolphins, there were a lot of them in the sea and many poor people would get some money.

"Well, dolphins are very intelligent animals," Jules said. "We don't think they should be captured and made to perform for people. They're taken away from their pods—their families—and some of them die."

"That going on in Jamaica?" Lloyd asked.

"The traders aren't Jamaican—it's illegal to catch a wild dolphin in Jamaica. The traders are from all over the world, but they come to the islands, including here, and they pay fishers to catch dolphins for them."

"Why them don't catch them in their own countries?"

"Because law enforcement is better there and the penalties are high."

"What happen after the dolphins get catch?"

"They put them on a plane or a boat and sell them. A healthy, young dolphin is worth a lot of money."

Lloyd thought of the folded bills in his father's hand. "You know who is doin it in Jamaica?"

"We don't know for sure," said Madison. "We've heard one name, an alias—Black Crab. You know someone with that name?"

Lloyd stared at her. "Not everything good to talk, Miss," he said.

"What?" she said, turning to Jules.

"He's telling you that trying to find out who Black Crab is might be risky."

Madison shrugged. Lloyd could see she felt safe in her white skin. He wondered about her life, but it was too foreign to him. He didn't know how to explain the dangers to these two women.

He remembered the last time he had gone fishing with Gramps, a week before the old man had left for Pedro, and on that morning even he had not landed many fish—only three red snapper, the biggest one not five pounds. Maas Conrad had stared at the fish in the old cooler and said to his grandson that fish-nin was dying, that no one could make a decent living anymore.

He told Lloyd things he already knew: how the fishers had to go farther and farther out to sea to catch the same amount of fish, but how the fish were different. They were trash fish, hardly any grouper and red snapper and yellowtail and even the parrot fish were smaller and smaller. Lloyd thought of the oily fish tea that was made with the trash fish, how it tasted of fish that had been dead too long. Gramps told how the price of gas kept going up, how the boats and engines were old and falling apart, how the uptown supermarkets were full of foreign fish in Styrofoam containers. As he talked, it seemed as if he had forgotten Lloyd was in the boat with him. "A man has to do *somethin*," he said.

Gramps said some men turned to selling drugs, buying cocaine from boats coming from Colombia, heading for Miami, and then selling the cocaine to the local dons, who in turn exchanged the drugs for guns. He told how some men became thieves, pulling the fish pots set by good fishers; not the best, not the most experienced pot fishers, because those men set their pots without floats and ropes, so no one could find them. Other men became pirates, raiding the boats of fishers, stealing catch and equipment and cell phones and money at the point of a gun. Some fishers became desperate as the demands of their baby mothers mounted, causing violence in homes and in yards and in the rum shops. They got sticks of dynamite from the police, or chlorine from a bredren at the chemical company on the Boulevard, and that was how they fished. They could not afford to waste any time thinking about any other day except the day in front of them. It was the longest speech Lloyd had ever heard from his grandfather.

He turned to the two women, who were still waiting for him to speak. "I heard that name," he said. "Black Crab."

"Can you help us find him?" asked Madison.

"Mebbe," he said.

The men of Great Bay half carried Luke to our house and the women became businesslike. Miss Adina bustled off to make chicken soup, Miss Faith to find sinkle bible—aloe— to soothe Luke's scorched skin, Miss Olga to convince Pastor Peter to keep a special service. Luke had still not opened his eyes, but he had lifted his hands and now held the cup. I touched his bare arm and it felt like the baked earth left behind when the pond dried up, as if his skin might crack and blow away on the sea breeze. I saw the shape of his skull and the long bones of his limbs and the rounded clumps of his joints, like marbles in a bag. Eight, nearly nine days at sea.

At home, my mother bathed her son and anointed his limbs with the cool jelly of the sinkle bible plant. She oiled his lips with Vaseline. She dressed him in clean shorts and led him to her own bed. She spread a towel on top of the sheets and he lay down like an old man. She sat beside him. We others hovered in the room like duppies—ghosts. We heard Miss Adina arrive and the clink of pots and spoons and bowls, the things of land. Miss Adina brought a bowl of chicken soup to my mother. It hot, she said, and fresh. And me cut up the chicken fine-fine. My mother blew on the soup and she held Luke's head up, and she fed him, one small spoonful at a time. I thought again of birds. He did not finish the bowl. When it was about half done, he turned his head away and my mother let him sink into the bed. He closed his eyes. I was afraid to see him sleep, afraid that after his ordeal and his final long journey to land, he would die in his own home. We stood and watched him, marking every twitch of his eyelids, welcoming the sound of his drawn breath. Let him sleep, my mother said, and we left the room one by one.

My brother had come home. And I had not eaten for a day. I wanted his soup.

Robert arrived with a woman he knew from Southside; she was a nurse, he said. The clinic in Black River would not send a doctor to Great Bay—we would have to take Luke to them. *The woman held Luke's wrist and looked at a watch she took out of her pocket. She laid her palm on his forehead. The main thing, she said, is to get him to drink. Coconut water is best.*

I ate a big bowl of soup and half a loaf of hard dough bread. I put on clean, dry clothes. My mother sat at the table with her head in her hands and she sobbed and prayed, thanking Jesus for her son's return. I tiptoed into my parents' bedroom. Luke had not moved. He looked as if he had been laid out in death. I watched his chest rise and fall. Then I left to find coconuts for my brother.

25

That same afternoon, Lloyd went back to the Tun-Up rum shop. He left the two women at Morgan's Harbour Hotel with promises to ask around for Black Crab, but he wanted to talk to Maas Roxton. He was upset with himself for not thinking of Gramps's old friend first.

Miss Violet was getting ready for the evening rush. She looked up when he came in and greeted him. "Evening, Miss Violet," he replied. "How I can get to Rocky Point? I want talk to Maas Roxton."

"Good idea, Lloydie. Me don't see him come this way long time, but him and you granddaddy was always close. You know Django?"

"The taxi man?"

"Ee-hee. Him have a woman in Rocky Point—him go there all the time. Bet you him will take you for a small money."

"Thanks, Miss Violet, me will ask him."

"Go check the Harbour View gas station. That's where him hang out. You a good boy, Lloydie," Miss Violet said and she smiled at him.

Lloyd walked along the hard gray sand at the edge of the sea, turning his back to the sunset. He could see the colors of the sky in the water. Suddenly, he longed to be at sea. His trip on the Coast Guard boat seemed months ago. He wanted to be in a fishing canoe, even if it was not *Water Bird*. He wanted to carry out familiar tasks of casting a line or pulling a fish pot, he wanted the sea breeze in his face, to be free of the land. He stepped around one of the round jellyfish that were common in Kingston Harbour, avoiding its stinging tentacles.

Night came. He thought briefly of the wall on Gray Pond beach, of his wait for his grandfather, his role as sentry, as witness—but he was too tired and his grief hurt. He left the beach and walked home. He would look for Django the next day.

Django's taxi was an old Toyota Corolla. It was closing on midday before they left Harbour View, with Lloyd in the back between two women. Another friend of Django's sat in the front. Lloyd held no particular hope.

"How long to Rocky Point?" he asked Django.

"Mebbe three hours," Django said.

They drove through Kingston traffic onto the Mandela Highway and through Spanish Town. One of the women got off and Django waited in a gas station for another fare. Lloyd closed his eyes. He hoped he would get to Rocky Point before nightfall.

He woke when the taxi fell into a deep pothole and Django swore. They were driving through cane fields. "Soon reach now," Django said.

"When you going back?"

"Early tomorrow. 'Bout five-thirty. Need to beat the traffic into town. You comin?"

"Dunno. Tell me where you leavin out from and if you see me, you see me."

Django took Lloyd straight to Maas Roxton's small concrete house on the edge of a salt pond. There were other similar houses scattered around. The yard was dirt. Clothes flapped on a line. Lloyd estimated it was close to four o'clock. He walked up to the front door and knocked. There was no answer. He sat on the front step. He would just have to wait. People walked past on the marl road and looked at him waiting but no one said anything. After an hour, he saw the old man coming up the road. Lloyd stood.

"That you, Lloydie?" said Maas Roxton, limping into the yard.

"Ee-hee."

"Him dead, Lloydie? Is that you come tell me? Me know, yout', me know."

Lloyd held his breath. "You see him dead?"

"Me no see him, but . . . come inside. Not good to talk these things where man can hear."

Lloyd followed the old man into the house. The small dwelling had almost no furniture, and fishing gear and engine parts were scattered around. It was more storage space for fishing gear than a home. It was very hot inside. "Sit," Maas Roxton said. Lloyd sat on a broken couch covered in plastic near the only window. At least he would soon know what had happened to his grandfather. It had been a very long day and he was weary.

At first, Luke only slept, ate, and drank. He used the chamber pot—the chimmy—and my mother studied the contents before she emptied it. The color of Luke's urine changed from a rusty brown to pale yellow. My mother waited for him to move his bowels. That took days. His skin sloughed off in big flakes. He spoke in monosyllables and only about food or water. I climbed every coconut tree in the four villages of Treasure Beach and brought the nuts home in clusters and Luke drank the water and ate the jelly. The pale, sandy color of the grass in Treasure Beach turned green and shining after the rain, and water rose in the pond.

My mother moved a chair from the big room and one of us sat in the bedroom with Luke, day and night. We slept where we could find space. At the time, the hours Luke lay still in bed seemed endless—but now, I know my brother recovered quickly. Soon he needed no help to use the chimmy. Soon he was ravenous—he ate brown stew chicken, curry goat, oxtail, rice and peas, roast breadfruit, sweet potato pone, bulla, boiled yam, even steamed fish and mackerel run down. I had thought he would turn away from all things of the sea, but he did not.

He could not stand his mouth to be empty. Miss Faith brought him a bag of the hard sticky sweets we called Bustamante Backbone and he sucked on them through all his waking hours.

What happen? we asked. Where you were?

Luke's story emerged. It had been a mistake to go to sea with Donovan—he had carried a full bottle of white rum and had drunk it all on the outward journey. They had spent three days on Top Cay, finding meager shelter in an abandoned shack. Donovan had refused to go to sea and Luke had set his pots alone. Then they waited and Donovan cursed the sea and the small coral island and threatened to kill everyone and everything on Top Cay—the men, the birds, the turtles that came to land at night to lay their eggs. An elder, Maas Leroy, told

Luke he had to leave. Luke argued with Donovan, who did not want to help him draw his pots, but eventually he agreed and they set out at dawn of the fourth day.

The pots were full and Donovan became exuberant. They filled the plywood iceboxes of the packer boats that took fish from the Pedro Cays to mainland fishing villages with red snapper and grouper and lobster and parrot fish. As the full weight of the sun fell on the sea, they left for Great Bay with money in their pockets and a small amount of fish for their families.

Me open the throttle wide, Luke said, and the sea flat calm and we going be home in four hours, the most.

But two hours into the journey the engine died and they could not get it started. What had seemed a flat calm sea held a deep, irresistible surge and they were pushed and pushed to the southwest. Here Luke stopped his account and his eyes became vacant. We ate the raw fish, he said, but it rot fast. Most of it we throw in the sea and the sharks come. We drank the water, but we never bring enough and Donovan finish it the first night. It never rain. Donovan die on the sixth morning, just after sunrise. Him jump overboard and he go straight down. He don't even come up to take one breath.

After he was alone, my brother spent his days lost at sea wedged in the small V-shaped shade of the bow cap. He said he could hear the sea talking to him through the hull of the boat. He said birds pitched on the boat and he knew they were waiting for him to die so they could peck at his eyes. He never used the word "loneliness" but that is what I could feel—the desolation of being alone on the sea in a boat without power.

On the eighth night, he crawled out and looked at the sky. He said he knew he would die the next day when the sun came up. He was tired of trying to catch fish or birds or turtles. He *was tired of praying for rain. It was over. And then he thought of the fuel in the engine and in his mind he saw fishers leaving Great Bay in the dark. When he saw the first faint tinge of gray in the sky, he poured the fuel on the surface of the sea and he lit it with a match. That is how he was found by Maas Peter, who saw the glow of burning fuel in the fading night.*

26

Maas Roxton brought Lloyd a cup of water and sat opposite him on a chair. "Me sorry, Lloydie. Me know you and you granddaddy was close." He shook his head. "Is just a dangerous time now, and him is—was—one ignorant old fool. Man can really get himself kill over a *dolphin*?"

So here was the truth. Why hadn't he come to find Maas Roxton earlier? Why had he wasted time with the Coast Guard boat and the dolphin women? He faced the old man. "Tell me what happen," Lloyd said. The wondering would soon be over. "Why him go to Pedro? Him never go there in him life. What him go there for?"

"Him go 'cause him see you father catchin dolphin for the foreign people."

"*My* father?" Lloyd asked the question, but he felt he had

always known Vernon had something to do with Maas Conrad's disappearance.

"Ee-hee. Vernon. Your daddy. Conrad tell me one early mornin him comin home from a quick trip and him see Vernon with some other man. Them was loadin a dolphin into a pickup on Gray Pond beach. Him and Vernon did have words." Maas Roxton stopped.

"Me know Gramps love dolphin, but is not the first time him and Pa have words. Them have words all the time. What happen after that?"

"Maas Conrad find out 'bout some big crackdown on the Pedro Cays, environmental people want stop night fish-nin and spear fish-nin and government bring in some kind of fish sanctuary place where no fish-nin allow. And the Coast Guard catch some fisher with one whole heap a cocaine, and some other boat with a pile of shark fin. Then two conch compressor diver dead from stayin down too long. Me no know the whole story. But plain and straight, the government stop the fishers from do what them used to do and them stop make money. So them start catch dolphin and sell them to the foreign dolphin people. Been going on for a while near Negril, but not so easy to find dolphin along the north coast 'cause the reef dead and the fish small and dolphin not there more than so. So them start catch them out at Pedro."

"So Gramps go Pedro. For what?"

"Lloydie, me beg him don't go. Him leave from here, y'know. But you know how him stay. Him get worse the older him get, all him can chat 'bout is how the sea is mashin up and how all of we is to blame. Them kinda thing. You memba how him nearly get kill last year out by Old Harbour after him try beat up that police, what him name again? Aaahm . . ." The old man stopped and Lloyd wanted to say, who cares about the policeman. He waited.

"Corporal Armstrong. Yeh. Him sell dynamite to fishers."

"Me never know 'bout that."

"Conrad nearly get kill! Is only him gray hair save him. Corporal Armstrong say him never want see him again in Old Harbour." Maas Roxton sighed. "Me know why him go Pedro, but me don't know what him think him go do when him get there."

"So why you think him dead?"

"Him dead because a bad man say him must dead."

"Black Crab, you mean?"

"What you know 'bout Black Crab?" Maas Roxton looked terrified. "Lloydie you can't mix up-mix up inna these things. A big man thing. Bad man thing."

"Where I can find him?"

"You no hear what me just say, bwoy?"

"Me have to find him. You think Gramps dead but you no know for sure. Right? Right?"

"Lloydie, I know it hard. But is, what, ten days now since Conrad leave from Pedro. Him must dead. Black Crab send man to get rid of him. Me know that. Black Crab come here, him come to Rocky Point and Welcome Beach and Old Harbour and him tell everybody to keep them mouth shut, that dolphin business a good business, and how nuff man eatin a food from it, and how one old man nah go stop it with him fool-fool chat. How dolphin just a fish, just one animal, like any animal, and what, we must stop eat chicken, stop jerk pork, nobody must have curry goat feed? Not a manjack agree with that. Not a man think anything wrong with catchin a dolphin. After we all catch fish, no so?"

"Dolphin not a fish," Lloyd said.

"Same damn foolishness. Get it outta you head, yout'. I know it hard, no funeral, no proper nine night, but you granddaddy gone."

"Who Black Crab send to Pedro to find Gramps?"

"Me no know, Lloydie. Me know you father big up inna the dolphin business, but me no know if is him. Me not sayin is him. But me hear from 'nuff Pedro man that Vernon was out there—and him no like go sea more than so, you know that. If him was on Pedro, him go there for a reason."

"You look for him, Maas Roxton? You go look for you friend, for you bredren?" Lloyd stood. He wanted to hit the old man, to throw the cup he held against the wall.

"Don't facety to me yout'. You is outta order. Is not you one care about you granddaddy. But me have grandpickney too and it nah go help them to bury me, you hear? Yes, me look for him. Me look for him every time me go sea, me look for him at Hellshire and on Pigeon Island and on Pelican. But is a big sea. Me don't find him. Me know the Coast Guard look too."

"You see his boat?"

"Not a trace. Him gone, Lloydie. It hard, but him gone. You go home now and you forget 'bout it."

Lloyd walked to the door and stopped on the doorstep. He did not know what to believe.

"Where you going now, Lloydie?" Maas Roxton said. "You can't go back to town 'til tomorrow. Stay here tonight. I have some fish and festival, Miss Janet over by the Co-op fry it up for me. We beg a call over at the shop and tell you mother where you is. You get up early and go home with Django—is him bring you, don't it? Or you can come sea inna the mornin with me. We take some fish for Miss Beryl."

Lloyd's eyes filled with tears. It would be so good to cry, to mourn, to admit defeat.

"C'mon, Lloydie, you just a bwoy. Hear what me is tellin you."

Lloyd nodded slowly and he felt his body soften, and together the boy and the old man went in search of a cell phone with credit.

Luke stayed at home for three weeks. My family dispersed. Robert went back to Southside, Colin to Top Hill, Lewis to Billy's Bay, Ben to Junction. My father went to Black River. My mother cleaned and cooked. I waited. When Luke took his first steps around our house I walked beside him. I watched his flesh fill out and soften the hard lines of his bones. He was still hungry and he drank a whole coconut every single hour he was awake. People from the community came by, mostly the women, and they brought gifts—a special oil for the skin, a tea that would bring sleep and a quiet mind, sweet potatoes just dug from the earth. No one spoke the words we were all thinking—would Luke go to sea again?

At night, I lay on the floor on my pile of blankets and listened to my brother's breathing and I thought about a life on the sea, the life of a fisher. When the fish were biting, we had money. We had respect. We were big men in the community. If we were lost, a search was mounted and the whole community waited for our return. I had no other trade. Until Luke went to drift, I thought I knew the sea. I thought often about what he said, that the sea talked to him through the thin hull of the boat, and as I lay on the floor I listened for the words of the earth below me but it was silent.

I knew I would go to sea again. Never with a man like Donovan, never if the weather was bad, never if something simply did not feel right. And never to the Pedro Bank. I would never take the journey all my brothers had taken, never see the man with two rows of teeth like a shark, never sleep and wake on a cay in the middle of the Caribbean Sea. But I would go to sea, I would come home to land at the edge of the sea, but the sea was and would always be my world and my work.

In the fourth week after Luke's return, our father came up to us where we sat on the front steps, Luke with a coconut shell in his hands. Tomorrow, he said to Luke. You be ready. My brother nodded.

Me can come? I said.

My father pursed his lips and looked down. Ee-hee, he said eventually.

The next morning we skimmed over a light chop into the whorls of sunrise and Luke took his place at the bow, holding the anchor rope, riding the eternal power of the sea. And that morning we saw the dolphins at the reef; we saw a female with her calf and a big male that rode our bow wave, close enough to touch. It was a morning of triumph and I grinned at Luke. I loved dolphins anew. All my life they reminded me of the day I made my peace with the sea.

I know I will die on this rock in the sea. There is no escape. A man born to drown cannot hang. The Pedro Bank has been waiting for me.

27

The next morning, Maas Roxton and Lloyd left to pull pots. The weather was dull and sticky and the choppy sea held a threat of something more. Lloyd had fallen asleep on an old army cot as soon as he had eaten and had slept deeply and dreamlessly all night. Yet he felt heavy. Maas Roxton said his grandfather was dead. Perhaps it was time to accept it.

"We go over by Wreck Reef," Maas Roxton said. "Then to Gray Pond. You sell some fish, you pray for you granddaddy and you go about you business after that, seen, Lloydie?"

They left the cays of Portland Bight and the town of Old Harbour and the round dome of Rocky Point behind and Maas Roxton kept *Testament* close to the coast, past Coquor Bay and Manatee Bay. When they reached Needles Point, Lloyd looked over at Tern Cay and tried to think when last he had visited Tern Cay with his grandfather—it must have been at least three months ago, perhaps in his Easter holidays.

He watched the coastline slip by. There were beaches fringed with mangroves in some places, in other places it was rocky and a boat without power would be dashed to pieces by the surf. Behind Wreck Reef, the sea was calmer. They headed to the first pot and began to draw it, working in silence. Lloyd remembered the story of the dolphins leading Gramps through the dangerous coral heads of Wreck Reef and he was angry at his grandfather for telling him such tales. There were no miracles.

The fishing was poor and Maas Roxton's traps held very little of value. "Sea gettin up," he said. "Time to call it a day." His catch would not pay for the fuel to take Lloyd home. They left the Hellshire coast and headed for Kingston Harbour. When they entered the Harbour, Maas Roxton opened the throttle and *Testament* raced across the sea. They passed the Coast Guard base. *Surrey* was not at anchor.

"You fish at Pedro?" Lloyd asked Maas Roxton over the noise of the engine.

"Yeah, sometime. Fish-nin much better than 'round here, but is a long boat ride."

"Suppose somebody hurt Gramps. Suppose him in the sea. Him swim good, you know. Where him could wash up out there, where nobody would find him?"

"Bwoy, Lloydie, you head tough like a dry coconut. Three cays on Pedro—Top, Middle, and Bird Cay. Man live on Top and Middle—you know that. Nowhere to hide there."

"What about Bird Cay?"

"Nobody live there, but you can see it easy, and fishers go there all the time. Although, mark you, now Bird Cay is in the fish sanctuary and nobody not supposed to be over there except the wardens."

"Maybe Gramps is there then."

"Lloydie, if him is on Bird Cay, and him stand on the beach and wave him hand, everybody see him. Him can't be there. If him is there, him is dead."

"Nowhere else on Pedro him could be?" Lloyd saw the cranes of Gordon Cay and the power plant and the refinery and the tall buildings of downtown Kingston ahead. He saw the fishing boats gathered at the old sewage plant outfalls. He was nearly home.

"Well, I suppose a man could drift to Portland Rock, but him can't survive there, not for long. No shade, no water, nuttn but bird nastiness."

"Where is Portland Rock?"

"Pedro. Two hour from Middle Cay. In the north. Depend where him did go into the sea as to whether him could end up there."

Lloyd had never heard of Portland Rock. "What it look like?"

"Me only go there once. Is just a rock sticking outta the sea. What you want me tell you? Is a big rock. Sharp. Easy to cut you. Nuff bird and crab. If it rain, water collect in the hole in the rock. Me think the bird like that. Windward side rough as hell."

"Nobody is there?"

"Sometime fishers camp out there. Them don't stay long. No fresh water, like me say. Only one place a boat can land. Water pretty, though—blue and deep and clean. Nuff shark too. That's another thing. How a man could swim through the whole heap of shark?"

"Me going look," said Lloyd.

Maas Roxton cut the engine and they glided onto Gray Pond beach. "Lloydie, what me must do with you?" he said. Lloyd said nothing. They faced each other, the old man with his hand still on the tiller and the boy sitting astride one of the thwarts. Maas Roxton sighed. "Awright. Is on you own head. Better you look for Black Crab than go Portland Rock. You no see the sky? Storm a come. Crab hang out at a bar name Shotta near Newport West. Maybe him feel sorry for a yout'. Me hope so, anyway."

"Thanks, Maas Roxton. Me have to try."

"Take these two parrot fish for Miss Beryl, youngster. Take them. Me want you to eat good tonight. Me sorry . . ." His voice trailed off.

"You know anybody will take me to Portland Rock?" Lloyd said.

Maas Roxton sighed. "You going search the whole sea, Lloydie?"

"He could be there."

"Eleven days on a rock inna the sea. No food? No water?"

"If it rain, why not? If bird and crab is there, why not? Maybe fishers leave a tent." Lloyd stopped. "You ever see dolphins out there?"

"You and the blasted dolphins. Me never see them the day me go, but fisher talk about them out there."

"Plenty a them?"

"Me no know, Lloydie. What a crosses! Anyway, me done. Me tell you what me know. Me sure Conrad is dead. That's it. You stay away from all the dolphin business or you be the next one nobody know what happen to. You get between a man and his bread, somebody go get hurt. Tell Miss Beryl how-de-do, awright?"

"Ee-hee. Thanks, Maas Roxton." Lloyd watched the old man stumble across the sand. Gramps was old, but he was strong; stronger than his friend. Lloyd was sure he could have climbed up onto Portland Rock. He would find his way to the rock in the sea, but not until he had spoken to Black Crab. He would ask Dwight to go with him to find the bar called Shotta near to Newport West.

I think this is my eleventh day on Portland Rock, but I am no longer sure. The rock pools are empty of water now. The plastic bottle is quarter full. There is not a single sea snail near to me. I should have eaten the ones farther away when I was stronger. I am afraid to stand again. Soon I will not be able to crawl. I am no longer hungry but my thirst burns and burns. I live in my memories; they make the hours pass and the pain in my leg bearable.

I remember the loss of Snowboy *in the 1960s, how the communities mourned and how a fund was set up by our prime minister, Alexander Bustamante, and how the discussions were about which children should benefit from the fund as the men who were lost at sea had more than one family. That was the first time I heard the word "illegitimate." Once the fund was started, the lost fishers were forgotten, their lives exchanged for money. I always wondered who owned* Snowboy *and whether they continued to send boats full of fishers to sea. By then my parents were both dead, my father of some wasting sickness no one ever named, a skeleton in the Black River Hospital, his skin turned from black to gray.*

Only Luke and I were still in Great Bay when Snowboy *went to drift. We lived in our old house, me with Jasmine, Luke with Cordella, who I never liked. By then, we were going farther and farther to catch the same amount of fish. It was hard to make ends meet.*

I remember the rains from Hurricane Flora when the pond overflowed into all the houses that had been built too close. Only the lignum vitae trees held firm—the coconut trees were uprooted, every last one. We lost our roof and nearly all our possessions. The farms of St. Elizabeth were washed away. It rained for weeks and the land turned a strange, unnatural green. Goats died from eating the acid green grass. The sea was churned up and fishing was bad. It was then that Jasmine's old desire for Kingston took hold of her.

28

Lloyd and Dwight made their way to Newport West next day. Lloyd told himself he was on a quest. His sidekick was Dwight. Black Crab would know where he could look for Gramps. And if it was Portland Rock, he would go there next.

The Shotta bar was a plywood structure with a slanted tin roof, like a lean-to. Dancehall music throbbed from two large speakers on either side of the bar. Two old men with lowered heads sat on bar stools. Beyond them, a fisher worked on a fish pot under a sea grape tree. There was no beach.

The barman had reddened eyes. Lloyd ordered a Pepsi in two cups without ice and the barman brought them. The boys sat at the bar and looked around. Apart from the two men at the other end of the bar, there was a thin black man sitting right in front of the speakers with a cell phone to his ear. He was dressed in torn jeans and an undershirt and another cell phone buzzed on a metal table in front of him.

"We ask the barman for Black Crab or what?" Dwight whispered.

"Shh! Just cool," Lloyd said. "Make us wait a little and see what happen."

Nothing happened. The man on the phone ended his call and wandered outside. The barman closed his eyes and his head fell forward. A mouse ran across the packed dirt floor. It was hot in the tiny bar—the sea breeze had not yet come up.

Lloyd rapped the bar and the barman jumped. "You know a man name Black Crab?"

The barman's head came up and he met Lloyd's eyes. "What you want with him? You not from 'round here?"

"Bournemouth," Lloyd said and instantly regretted it. It was best not to tell anyone where you lived. "Just want ask him a question, boss."

"Black Crab don't so much like question. But you young still. CRAB!" he shouted over the music. "This yout' here want a word."

The boys turned to see the thin black man who had been on the phone walking toward them. He did not look scary in the least. As he walked up to them, Lloyd saw he was older than he had first thought. He had a seagoing look around his eyes, which were scored with wrinkles. His arms were ropy, as if he spent hours drawing a net. His skin was black but it had the fisher's tinge of salt. "You askin for me, yout'?" His voice was soft but Lloyd heard an echo of menace in the simple words.

Lloyd slid off the stool and stood in front of the man called Black Crab. "Boss," he said. "Me is Lloyd. Lloyd Saunders. This my friend Dwight. We from over by Gray Pond fishin beach. Me—"

"How you come to be lookin for Black Crab?"

The truth or a story? Lloyd decided on the truth. "Me is lookin for my granddaddy, Maas Conrad him name. Him lost at sea. Him go the Pedro Cays, eleven day now, and him don't come back. Nobody heard from him. So—"

"What that have to do with me? Where you get my name from?"

"We hear," Dwight said. "We just ask around and we hear. We hear say you know about the foreign people what come here to buy dolphin. We hear you is a big man so we come find you."

Black Crab did not react to Dwight's voice. His eyes remained fixed on Lloyd, who became aware that the two old men were leaving the bar. The barman followed them, shaking his head. The music pounded and the bar was too dark. "Boss," Lloyd said. "Me don't mean no disrespect. Please. Me don't care if dolphin catch for whatever reason. Catch them all, me say, long as man can eat a food from it. But my granddaddy, him is an elder. Him hold to the old ways. All me want know is if him see sumpn him not suppose to see and if him is hurt somewhere, alone somewhere. That's it. It don't go no further than me and Dwight. Me can't hurt you, me know how to keep my mouth shut. Me is not a informer." Lloyd stopped. He had not said the right words, the words that were in his heart. Is he dead? Will his body ever be found? Will I ever know who killed him?

Black Crab stared into Lloyd's eyes. "Informer to dead. Right, yout'?"

Lloyd nodded. No one spoke and the music blared. Finally, Black Crab said, "Where you granddaddy fish from?"

"Gray Pond beach. That's where him keep his boat."

"What him boat name?"

"*Water Bird.*"

"You have a cell?"

"No, boss."

"WINSTON!" Black Crab bawled and the barman came running over. "Pass a paper and pen." Winston looked under the counter and Lloyd saw his hands were trembling. He handed over an exercise book of the kind the boys used in school and a ballpoint pen. Black Crab tore out a piece of paper and wrote on it shaking the pen to make it write. "This my number. Call me in a week—"

"A week!" Lloyd said. "Suppose him is hurt, starvin, no water, somewhere on the coast or lost in the boat with no engine."

"You love you granddaddy, yout'. That a good thing. Me did have a granddaddy too. Awright. You call me tomorrow. Then you throw away that paper. You forget the name Black Crab, you hear me? You go school, you play a little ball, you help you mother, you go sea, you do whatever you do. Me don't want see or hear from you again, seen?"

"Yes, boss. Thank you, boss," Lloyd said. "Tomorrow."

The boys turned to go. "Me can ask you one thing, boss?" Dwight said. Lloyd pinched his arm but the words were out.

Black Crab said nothing but his eyes narrowed and moved to Dwight's face. Lloyd was suddenly afraid for his friend. "Why them call you Black Crab?" Dwight asked.

The man called Black Crab laughed. "But see here now. Why you think? Them call me that 'cause me *love* eat black crab!"

We became poor. It seemed to happen overnight—smaller catches, the empty market. The two women squabbled day and night: who had lit a fire too close to the line of washing, who had failed to clean up after themselves, which man was the better fisher, whether or not the little money Luke and I brought home should be split equally. The house I grew up in became a place of strife.

And then Jasmine got pregnant. It was not an easy pregnancy—she vomited day and night for nine months. We were constantly at the Black River Hospital. We owed Maas Lenny for taxi fares we could not pay, the clinic was free but the medications were not. And the advice of the doctor was always the same—Jasmine needs good nutritious food, protein especially, and rest. My woman became thin with a round high belly like a smoothed beach rock. The schoolgirl who sat with me in the Arawak cave and held my hand was a flickering memory.

The fishing was especially bad after Hurricane Flora and the heat was a torment. I saw the reproach in Jasmine's eyes when catches were bad and we ate only rice or dumplings for supper, maybe with some pear when it was in season. Cordella swore at Luke and he stopped coming home. I went to sea alone and came back with a few small caesar fish, day after day. I did not know whether to sell the fish or give them to Jasmine to eat.

The word Kingston became a chorus in our house—Kingston-Kingston-Kingston. Jasmine said there were jobs in Kingston, opportunities, progress. And there was a harbor, Kingston Harbour, so if Luke and I were bound and determined to continue fishing we could do that. Maybe the fish were biting there. But the word Kingston always sounded heavy to me, like something falling, something that would do damage when it landed.

Then one day Luke came to me as I readied Silver for sea. Where you going? he said.

Guinea Shoal, I answered.

Don't make any sense. It fish out clean.

I shrugged. What else me going do? Plant skellion for Maas Gladstone? Cut bush for the Parish Council? Break stone for Public Works?

Luke looked behind him and dropped his voice. We need one good catch, he said. To tide us over 'til the fish start bite again.

Ee-hee, I said. Tell me sumpn me don't know.

He reached into his pocket and took out two sticks of dynamite. This is how we going get a good catch.

You lick you head? Where you get that?

Man in Alligator Pond. Them say them do it all the time. One time, bredren. One time.

I wished for my father then. He would tell us not to do this thing and we would listen. No, Luke, I said to my brother. But together we pushed Silver *into the sea.*

29

Lloyd spent the next morning in Liguanea with his mother, wrapping fish, thinking of Maas Conrad, Black Crab, and Portland Rock. He and his mother talked and the stiffness between them eased. "Gramps was from country, true?" he had said to his mother. Talking about his grandfather kept him alive.

"Ee-hee," she said. "St. Elizabeth parish. Treasure Beach. Great Bay." She stopped to deal with a customer. "I used to like country," she said, when she had finished.

"Which country?"

"St. Elizabeth."

"Same like Gramps?" His mother nodded. "But not near the sea. Your granny had a small farm near Lititz. Grew skellion and pumpkin. Used to go there in the summer."

"There was a river?"

"No river. We had to cut guinea grass to put around the plants to keep water in the dirt. Is a dry place, St. Elizabeth."

Lloyd knew his mother's mother had died when she was a young woman. "What happen to the farm?"

"Oh, one of the outside children got it. Was okay with me. Me was done with farmin by then. Fine when you is a pickney, runnin up and down inna the hot sun, but . . . "

Lloyd wanted to keep his mother talking. He racked his brain for a new subject. "You like being in Kingston then?" As soon as the words were out of his mouth, he knew how stupid they sounded, like something the son in an American family on TV might say.

Miss Beryl looked amazed. "If me like Kingston? What kinda question that? Me here. We here. Doing what we have to. That's it. Mornin, Miss," she said to one of the uptown people. "What for you today?"

They packed up at lunchtime. Without Maas Conrad's fish, they were making much less money. "Tomorrow," Miss Beryl said to her son. "Tomorrow this foolishness with your granddaddy is done, you hear me? You go sea. You bring home fish or money. Time for you to be a man."

Lloyd walked to Gray Pond beach. It was late afternoon and he hoped to find Maas Benjy or Maas Rusty under the divi-divi tree. Maybe one of them would have a cell phone with credit, so he could phone Black Crab. He was anxious. He wanted to know the truth, but he was afraid of it too. The shade under the divi-divi tree was empty and there were few people on the beach.

Lloyd walked east, facing the low sun. He passed the few vendors' shacks at the end of the beach. He saw Miss Violet from the Tun-Up rum shop leaning on the counter of one of the fish shops, chatting to the owner, Miss Selena. "Miss Violet, Miss Selena," he greeted them.

"Wha'appen, Lloydie?" Miss Violet said. "You hear from Maas Conrad?"

"No. Nuttn."

"Is what, a week now?"

"Eleven—no, twelve days."

"Um-hmm." Violet shook her head and said no words of hope.

"Miss Violet, you have credit on you phone? You think I could make a call?"

"You callin a girl, Lloydie?" Miss Violet and Miss Selena laughed. "I tell you, young bwoy these days, them good!"

Lloyd smiled as if they were right and took the phone she handed over.

"Don't stay too long," Miss Violet said.

He walked away from the women and sat on a rock. Maybe Black Crab would not answer, would never answer. The sun was going down and the gray waters of the harbor began to glow with its light. Another day over, pulling back like a wave. He fought back his sense of defeat, his fear. He called Black Crab's number, and heard him say, "Yes?"

"Boss. Is me, Lloyd, from Gray Pond fishin beach. Lookin for my granddaddy, Maas Conrad. You said you gonna ask around. You gave me you number."

"Yes-yes. Listen me, yout'. Two things. Number one: you

granddaddy not comin back. Is rough, life hard, but so it go. Him gawn and that is the end of it."

"Boss, wha . . . "

"Me say to listen. Number two: those two woman you talk to 'bout dolphin—you tell them from *me* is time to find some other line of work, seen? Argument *done*."

"Why you never tell me this at the bar?"

Black Crab swore. "You think me know every man go a sea? You think me know every starving fisher, every hustler inna Kingston? You ask me to find out, me find out."

"What happen to him, boss? Please, me is beggin you, just tell me what happen."

"Yout', you mix up inna big man business. Dangerous business. Lef' it alone now. You hear me? Or *you* the next one lost at sea, seen?"

Lloyd said nothing. He was tired of hearing that. He held the phone tightly and his palm was sweaty. He was alone on the beach, facing the harbor. "Yout'?" said Black Crab. "You still there? You hear what me say?"

"Yes, boss. Me hear."

"Tek care then, yout'. Tell the dolphin woman find sumpn else to do," Black Crab said. "And me don't want hear from you again. *Never,* you hear?"

Luke and I argued about using the dynamite as we pulled our pots and when we went home that night we carried only two juvenile yellow tails, wrapped in newspaper. Two small fish to feed four adults. I wanted to hide them from Luke and Cordella. I could cook them on the beach, get Jasmine out of the house; maybe Miss Adina would trust me two slices of hard dough bread and I would watch Jasmine eat. I thought about the Bible story of the feeding of the five thousand—five loaves and two small fishes. But there were no miracles to be had in Great Bay and I hated my willingness to take food from my brother. I had to do something—we had to do something. One time, I told myself.

The next morning Luke and I left Great Bay in the dark. It was rough and we fought our way through the waves. We were soaked as soon as we cleared the shelter offered by the curving coast. Silver swooped up and down, sometimes her engine racing when it was clear of the sea as she hung on the crest of a wave. Luke and I did not speak. We knew the fishers of Alligator Pond used dynamite. The fishers of our villages looked down on them for that because they did not commit such crimes.

When the sky lightened we were near our father's favorite pot set, on the reef where we set reef traps as boys, where we dove for conch and spearfished for lobster.

We do this before the sun come up, Luke said.

You know what you doing? I asked.

Yeah, man, he said. The man from Alligator Pond tell me.

I stared into the water. We right over the reef, I said.

Luke did not answer. He pulled the sticks of dynamite from his pocket and tried to light them but the matches were wet. Once, twice, the matches caught, sputtered, and died. Luke cursed and threw each dead match into the sea. I counted them, six, seven. I did not know if the pack of matches was full.

You have any newspaper? he said.

No, I replied.

Luke kept on striking matches. Eleven, twelve.

The fifteenth match caught and held and he shouted at me to help him. I cupped my hands around the tiny flame. It was such a fragile thing. The smallest of breaths would have blown it out, but I held my breath. Luke held one of the wicks to the flame and the flame danced with it. And then it caught. And the dynamite fizzed and I wondered how long it would take to explode and if perhaps this was how we would die, blown up by construction dynamite. Luke waited a long few seconds and then he threw it into the sea. At first nothing happened and then there was a crump and a swelling from the sea and then a white splash in the dark. Luke started the engine and we went to a second spot and this time the first match caught and Luke handed me the lit dynamite. Our eyes met—we were together in this. I threw the dynamite into the sea.

As the sky lightened, we saw what we had done. Fish of every size slid this way and that on the roiling sea, but not as many as I expected. I had thought the fish were there, just hiding in the reef; now it seemed they were not there at all. Bits of coral rose and sank. We scooped up the fish in dip nets taking no time to sort out the ones that were too small to eat. Some slid through the holes in the net.

The fish we took from the sea lay still in the bottom of the boat. There was no flapping, no fight for breath. There were few of any decent size. Then bigger ones started to float up and through my shame I felt relief. As I worked, I held Jasmine in my mind.

The sun rose and we rested. The bottom of the boat held fish and other things—eels and rays and pieces of sea fans. We going to take all these back? I said.

Why not? Small ones can make fish tea.

People going know about the dynamite if we take them all back.

Nobody care anymore, said Luke.

I wondered if this was so. I looked at the dead fish, a silvery mass with flashes of every single fading color, all killed in a few seconds, most of them what we would have called trash fish only a few years ago. They were whole and catching them had been much easier than fishing with pot or net or line. We would eat tonight and there would be money in our pockets. The laws of men had been broken, and that was bad, but we had also broken the laws of the sea, and that was worse.

Luke started the engine and just as we turned Silver *in the direction of Great Bay, just as the pink of sunrise faded from the sky, we saw what seemed to be a large log float to the surface. Wait, I said. What over there?*

Where? Luke said, looking in the direction I pointed. Shark, maybe.

He slowed and turned toward the thing the waves covered and revealed. I saw blood in the water. I saw an eye without brightness and a dead smile and I saw the sleek body of a young dolphin lying lifeless on the surface of the sea. Perhaps it was the calf we had once seen with its mother; that day, it was the dolphin Luke and I killed together.

30

One more place, Lloyd told himself. The sky burned in the west; night and bad weather were on their way. He borrowed Miss Violet's phone again and called Jules's number. She answered on the first ring.

"You ever been to Portland Rock?" he said.

"What? Who is this?"

"Miss Julie. Is me, Lloydie."

"Oh Lloydie. Jules, remember? How you doing? No news, huh? You find Black Crab yet?"

"You ever been to Portland Rock?" Lloyd said again, avoiding the question.

"I have. Good place for dolphins. That's where I do a lot of my surveys."

"Me think Gramps is there."

"Portland Rock? Why?"

"So me hear," he lied.

"Fishers go there. If he was there, somebody would have found him."

"Fisher not there all the time, though?"

"No, that's true. They can't stay for long. It's bare rock. No water. Nothing except birds."

"And crabs," he said, thinking about how an injured fisher would catch and eat a live crab.

"Yes, crabs too. But how long now since your granddaddy missing?"

"Soon be two weeks."

"That's a long time, Lloydie."

He wanted to shout at her, yes, I know is a long time! Stop tellin me that! Everybody, stop tellin me that. Is a long time but is not *eternity*. Is not *impossible*. He cast around for something to tell her that she would like, that she would believe.

"Miss. Make us go. Please. I want to see how you count dolphins. I want to be a scientist like you. And it will be the last place to look. I swear. After that I know Gramps dead. Please. Then I find Black Crab for you."

There was a silence. Lloyd hoped the credit on the cell phone would not run out. He was about to ask Jules to call him back, when she said, "Where are you?"

"Gray Pond beach."

"I had a trip planned for tomorrow morning. From Treasure Beach. Leaving Kingston in an hour. Can I talk to your mother? I don't want to take the responsibility for taking you with me without her permission."

Lloyd thought quickly. He needed a woman who would pretend to be his mother. "Awright, Miss. She sellin. Me will call you back and you can talk to her."

He went inside to Miss Violet. "Me know where him is Miss Vie! Me know. That woman, the one who study the dolphins, she go take me. But she want talk to my mother, you know how uptown people stay. You talk to her. Tell her you is my mother and is okay for me to go. Please. I am beggin you."

Miss Violet looked at him without expression. She wiped her face. She opened her mouth to speak and Lloyd interrupted her, "I know is a long time him gone. Don't tell me is a long time!"

"Aah, Lloydie. Not that me going say. Me going ask you if you sure you want find out what really happen."

"Of course me is sure! What kinda question that? Miss Vie, you know Gramps. Him is a tough old man. Him not go dead so easy. You know that."

"Man is just flesh and blood, Lloydie. Man is cruel. Life cruel. The sea cruel. It easy to die."

"Please, Miss Vie. Say you is my mother. This uptown woman, she not go to sea without everything, everything—life jacket, radio, GPS, two engines at least, extra fuel, flares. Everything. You know how it to. It going be safer than what I do every day of life."

Miss Violet considered. And then she said, "What she name?"

Jasmine had a son after a short sharp labor in the house in Great Bay attended by a midwife from Black River. We named him Vernon, after her father. She lost interest in me. The two women still fought and the house closed tight around us, unpleasant with Vernon's bawling and his smells and needs. I was not needed. We were living on what Luke brought in from dynamite fishing and I was not going to sea.

Luke quickly learned that our first efforts at dynamite fishing had been done all wrong. You were supposed to go at dusk on a calm day. You did not go to a random spot over the coral reef and take what floated up. You went to a place where fish schooled and you attracted them with bait or chum, and then you threw the dynamite. Luke became expert. I did it that one time only and ever after we were divided, almost enemies. Yet still I ate Luke's fish.

We never talked about the day we first threw explosives into the sea, but when Vernon was six months old, Jasmine, the baby, and I left Great Bay and moved to Kingston. She had a cousin in Gray Pond, a fishing beach just like Great Bay, she told me, although she had never seen it, with a pond like ours. I could not imagine a fishing beach in a city. Perhaps I would get construction work.

When we packed up all we owned I was surprised how small a pile it was. I said good-bye to Luke on the front steps of the house I had grown up in; Cordella was in the kitchen and did not come out. I knew she was glad the house would be hers alone. Maas Leroy took us in his taxi to Kingston and I looked back at the coastline only once at the top of the escarpment. I lived on an island and the sea would always be there, and it would always be the same sea, whether or not I was a fisher. I was twenty-five years old.

31

Jules shook her head when she saw Lloyd, sitting on the sidewalk of Windward Road, waiting for her. He had not been home. "Lloydie," was all she said. She handed him a plastic bag full of sandwiches and an icy Pepsi. He ate the sandwiches—bully beef, with just the right amount of pickapeppa sauce and Scotch bonnet—and he found every leftover crumb with his tongue. "Stretch out in the back," Jules said. "Go to sleep. It will take us a good three hours to get to Treasure Beach." Lloyd crawled into the back seat, lay his head on his backpack, and was instantly asleep.

Pressure in his bladder brought him awake. He was stiff, but he felt rested and strong. He was still thirsty. The sun was setting and they were driving down a winding road, the sea ahead of them far below. The soil was reddish with rocky outcrops and the grass was rough and gray. "Miss? We can stop for a minute?" he asked.

Jules pulled over beside a large limestone rock. Lloyd got out and relieved himself against a fence post. When he had finished, he looked out to the coastline. The hill they were on fell to a large flat plain containing a huge pond. Straggly trees leaned all one way. There was a large hill on the coast to the east. He could see the small houses of a village. "Where is that, Miss?" he said.

"Treasure Beach," she said. "That's Pedro Bluff. And the Great Pedro Pond. The Pedro Bank is out to sea. All these places named for someone called Pedro. We leave before first light. You alright? You feel better?"

"Yes, Miss." He caught a glimpse of what seemed to be a cave in the limestone outcrop off to one side and a faint path leading to it. He saw a small tree had sent its roots right into the rock and its roots framed the entrance to the cave. He turned his gaze to the sea. He was anxious to get down to the coast. He would tell Jules about Black Crab's warning; of course he would. As soon as they came back from Portland Rock, he would tell her. She had been going there anyway. It would not be any more dangerous than her regular trips.

Portland Rock. A dry breeze has torn half of the tarpaulin away and I can see the other half will follow. Then I will lie fully exposed to the sun and my life will be soon over. My leg pounds ceaselessly, like the sea itself. The rocks are full of the skeletons and marks of sea creatures—will I one day become one of these marks? They are like the pencil drawings we had to do at Sandy Bank primary school so many years ago. Will some future visitor see the faint traces of a man imprinted in rocks? Despite my long determination to avoid this place I am going to die alone on the Pedro Bank.

I hear the soft breath of dolphins nearby and they are a comfort. They came after the last rain and they have stayed. A crab runs across my leg. I think of the one I ate when I was first here. It was a female—her underside held reddish eggs. I ate them all. I smashed her shell. I never caught another crab.

There are piles of human excrement nearby. My hope has been focused on them. A few were fresh when I came here, but now they have dried. Surely, I thought for many days, the person who squatted on this rock will return.

I see Hatuey in my dreams. He speaks to me sometimes and he tells me of a sea so bountiful that his people caught fish in their hands by diving in the underwater caves of Great Bay; how, then, a man who could hold his breath for a long time was a big man. He explains how to tell time with the span of a hand held up between the arcing sun and the line of the horizon. He talks about the great wave that killed his people. He tells me to lay my hand on my navel—for the dead have no navels—it is the connecting place of the living body to the living world. And I feel it, the tides of the sea in my own blood, in that beginning place of connection to my mother, but I know the tide of my blood is ebbing.

32

They spent the night at a guesthouse. Jules requested a room with twin beds, which opened onto a small veranda. There was even a kitchen and a bathroom. Lloyd wanted to explore the community, but Jules said he should stay with her. They could walk down to a seafood restaurant for supper, she said. Then they would go through her gear. If he wanted to be a scientist, he might as well start learning right away. First, though, she wanted to just sit and watch the sun go down. Lloyd sat with her on the veranda and again noticed her ability to be perfectly still. He felt his blood was fizzing. The last thing he wanted to do was watch something that happened every day without fail. He looked at the sky for signs of weather, hoping for a fair morning the next day. He could not tell what the clouds held. The wind ceased and mosquitoes swarmed. Jules got up only when the last glow of evening died. "Come," she said. "Let's get some food."

The sounds of her preparations woke him in the night. "You up?" she said and turned on the light in the kitchen. She put a kettle on to boil and poured cereal from a box into bowls. All her gear was ready from the night before. "You use the bathroom first," she said.

Within an hour, they were at sea with Speedy, Jules's local guide. He was neither young nor old, and like most fishers Lloyd knew, a man of few words, but there had been a short discussion about the weather—Speedy thought there was a storm coming, but it was holding off. It would be a quick trip, Jules told him. Speedy did not want to wear the life jacket Jules held out to him and she insisted. It was obviously an argument they had had before. Eventually he slipped it on but refused to fasten it. Lloyd's life jacket was too big, but Jules cinched it tight around him.

"Straight to Portland Rock?" Speedy said.

"Uh-huh."

"How long?" Lloyd asked him.

"Three, maybe four hour," Speedy said. "Depend on the sea."

The boat, *Skylark*, was not large, but it was new and the white paint and chrome railings shone. It was much wider than a fishing canoe with a little shade canopy over the steering wheel. There were storage lockers under the bow, which held all Jules's gear. Four brand-new engines on the stern drove the boat through the water. There was a small seat in front of the wheel and Lloyd sat there with Jules, staring ahead into the night, waiting for sunrise.

Last night I dreamed of Jasmine and the bright round balls she wore in her hair when we were young. We did not do well in Kingston, she and I. For a while I worked on construction sites, shoveling gravel into a wheelbarrow. Carrying bags of cement. Mixing cement. Rendering cement. They called me unskilled and the pay was low. Jasmine worked at a haberdashery place on Orange Street until her boss told her she had to be his girlfriend. "No girlfriend, no job," he said. She left, but after that she could not find work. We were behind on the rent and the landlord shouted through the locked front door at night. If Vernon woke up, Jasmine put her hand over his mouth to keep him quiet, and I remember the gleam of his frightened eyes in the dark.

He was four when Jasmine left me for a soldier and took him with her. By then the only word she flung at me was: wut'less. The only sentence: you have no blasted use.

I went back to sea. I saw my son when she came on a Sunday to pick up her money. The money was never enough. The time I spent with Vernon was never enough. As he grew, he stared at me with anger. Jasmine began wearing a wig and her nails were long and dangerous.

Once a week, I borrowed the phone at the bar in Gray Pond and I spoke to Luke at Sheldon's Bar. We had little to say to each other, but I was glad to hear his voice. His news was always the same, times were hard, fish were few. Politics was mashing up everything. The men of Parotee near Black River fought with the men of Rocky Point and the fights continued out on the Pedro Cays. The white people who worked at the bauxite company in Mandeville bought land and built weekend houses. Calabash Bay was dying and the market was closed. The fishing beaches held many derelict and abandoned boats, once seaworthy, once cared for. There were more foreigners, and ganja was being exchanged for guns. Our brother Robert had left Jamaica for Honduras. More and more fishers built fish pots and sold them. More and more fishers were tied to land.

Luke asked me about the movie theaters and shops of Kingston but I had never been to those places.

The years passed. Luke and Cordella had no children. Luke said she was a mule. My brother had trouble remembering my son's name, calling him Vincent by mistake. Then one Sunday night Sheldon's son answered the phone and told me Luke was dead. Bwoy, me sorry, he said. Me sorry me have to tell you.

How him die? I asked. The dynamite kill him?

No, Sheldon's son said. Him die out a Pedro, compressor diving. That's where the money is now. The big thing is conch.

The Pedro Bank had claimed Luke after all.

33

Skylark headed southeast as the sun rose. The sky filled with streaks of color. Although the boat was new and modern, the hull slammed into the waves and they were all drenched. Every boat have it sea, Gramps used to say. Lloyd thought of his trip to Pedro on the *Surrey*, the long hours hidden under the dinghy in the dark. He smiled. Despite the heaving swells, his stomach was steady and he loved the breeze in his face. The life jacket warmed his body. Maybe his mother was wrong and he would be a fisher.

"How long now, Miss?" he asked Jules. She was wearing a wide-brimmed hat and holding a pair of binoculars in a plastic bag.

"Still a ways to go, Lloydie." She looked at her watch, and took out the binoculars. She looked through them in a wide sweep across the sea and then returned them to the bag. She made a mark on a plastic card. She did it again, about fifteen minutes later.

"What you doin, Miss?" Lloyd said.

"You want to be a scientist, this is what we do. I'm looking for dolphins, writing down whatever I see. Conditions are bad, though. I don't think we'll see any until we get close to Portland Rock."

"You write down that you don't see anything?"

"Sometimes nothing can tell you as much as something," she said. A big burst of spray came over *Skylark's* bow and they fell silent. I am comin, Lloyd said to his grandfather in his mind.

Another dawn. This one is spectacular and I am glad to see it unfold. Sometimes sunrise is a muted affair, at other times this brilliance, this celebration. I hear the clicking noises of crabs and the calls of gulls and the boom of the surf and the smaller splashes of pelicans diving for fish. The holes in the rocks are full of seawater again and the sky is clear. There will be no more squalls, at least not soon enough to matter. My mind is sharp even as my body shrivels. It is time to face what I remember about my journey to Portland Rock.

What were the chances of finding the dolphin catchers on the wide Caribbean Sea, on this piece of the whole earth rising from the seafloor, this Pedro Bank? The odds of finding my only son must have been the size of a grain of sand, one single grain of sand among uncountable millions—yet still I found him. I found him in the deep clear water near this rock where the dolphins come to feed and play. I found him and his bredren chasing them with banging pots and splashing oars into the nets they set. I found him because Slowly had told me where to go.

I was not afraid of Vernon nor the men with him, young and strong as they were. I wanted to ram their boats, but did not want to damage Water Bird. I pulled up beside them and I shouted at them. One of their boats circled away and I watched it. I did not see or feel whatever struck the back of my head, nor did I see who struck the blow. I did not see Water Bird float away.

I must have lost consciousness, for when I opened my eyes the sun was high. It was middle day and I was gone to drift without my boat. I floated face up on the surface of the sea and at first I could not understand why. Then I realized what had saved me—the life jacket I now lie on, a small softness between me and the rocks. All my life I wore my life jacket only intermittently, but on that last morning, when I left Middle Cay to find the place Slowly told me about, the place the dolphins were captured, I pulled it from under Water Bird's bow cap and put it on, grumbling to myself about the way it would make me hotter.

I turned in a circle, looking for boats. I was alone. I rose and fell in a shining sea with sharks all around and my blood in the water. I had never seen such clear water. I could see right down into it. The sharks were large—twelve, fourteen feet long. I felt no fear. Perhaps the blow made me lose a little of my mind. I hung in the water and tried not to move my arms and legs. Then I remembered something my father told me from his lifeguarding days—if you ever get stuck in the water with sharks roll up into a ball on the surface. You not going to look like food then and it will save your energy. Bobbing, he called it. I put my face in the water and felt the sting of salt on the back of my head. I felt for the wound—it was long but not deep. If this had happened on land I would have survived. I reached for my legs and curled into a ball.

It was hard to hold on to my legs in the ball shape, the life jacket was in the way, but it did keep me bobbing on the surface. As my father had shown me in my boyhood I turned my head to one side to breathe. I held my breath for the count of ten, and then I breathed. I kept my eyes open and the salt water stung. The blood in the water began to dissipate. I was drifting fast, carried by an unseen current.

I felt the brush of the big animals in the sea and the movement of the water as they circled beneath me, around me. My son had left me here to drown or be eaten by sharks. I wondered if he had been the man to strike me, or if he had merely watched. I could not understand why they had not killed me—they must have had guns. Even a spear gun would have done the job. Maybe they had argued about it, maybe my son had begged for me, and while they were shouting at each other, I had floated away on this current. Maybe they looked around at the expanse of the sea and shrugged—I was an old man, I was injured, and the water was full of sharks. Maybe they did not have the stomach for an execution. Maybe they just wanted to resume their hunt for the dolphins.

I felt the high sun beat on my neck. It was not feeding time for sharks unless they were very hungry. My head throbbed. The waves made me seasick. It seemed pointless to keep breathing but I found I could not simply stop. Water trickled into one ear and I started to turn my head to the other side.

Then I heard a soft wet exhalation beside me and then another and I knew at once the dolphins had come. I uncurled from the ball and lifted my head and they were all around me, some at the surface, others beneath me, some close, some far. I reached out to touch them but they instantly moved out of reach. I tried to swim along with them, my legs and arms flailing, the life jacket making me awkward in the sea. I saw the dolphins were moving in the direction of a sharp black rock, and I heard the flap of a tarpaulin or a sail, and there were many birds in the sky and then the dolphins dived and were gone.

There is not much left to tell. I pulled myself onto the rock—the sharp edges of the honeycomb rock were covered with the white droppings of seabirds. Everywhere I touched, I cut my skin—my fingers, my shins, my feet. On that first day and for a few days afterward, I could stand although I was dizzy and my legs were weak. I saw the signs of humans and I knew fishers used this place. They would come back. All I had to do was breathe and wait.

I found the flapping tarpaulin, which made a small patch of shade in a hollow and I stripped off the life jacket and lay on it. There was a bottle of water tied to a rock and I sipped from it. It was fresh, warm, and tasted of plastic but it would buy me some time, perhaps a week, more, if it rained. I closed my eyes then and I slept and I did not wake through that first night spent alone on Portland Rock on the Pedro Bank.

34

"See it there," Speedy said, and pointed.

They looked. Lloyd could just make out a long, low rock in the sea with two small craggy peaks. The waves seemed to surge over it completely and he could not see how anyone could survive there. Jules took out her binoculars and stared through them, balancing as the boat climbed the wave crests and fell into the troughs. "Think I see a tarpaulin. Maybe we can land on the lee side?" she said to Speedy and he nodded.

"Can I see?" Lloyd said.

Jules handed him the binoculars but everything was blurry. "Use this to focus," she said, turning a knob. The rock sprang into focus and it was bigger than he had imagined. He could see seabirds and sea spray but there was no sign of human life. "Go faster," he said to

Speedy, who did not reply. Jules reached for the binoculars, but he held on to them, looking for any sign of Gramps on Portland Rock.

The dark blue of the deep sea gave way to turquoise and Lloyd lowered the binoculars. The rock was much larger than it had appeared at a distance. The water was full of large sharks and the coral reef rose out of the deep and teemed with reef fish. He had never seen a sea like this, never in his life, a sea full of fish of every size and shape and color, a sea with water so clear it was hard to tell exactly where surface or seafloor was, a sea that seemed to merge with the air into one breathing world. A green turtle moved beneath *Skylark*, its flippers sweeping through the water in slow time.

Portland Rock loomed close now—low in the middle, higher at both ends, one end towering, and behind the highest peaks spray flew. They went around the rock to the leeward side and the sea calmed, but there was still the strong sea surge to contend with. And then Lloyd saw a canoe tied to a rock and his father's friend, Selvin, sitting on the rock. He stood as they approached. There was no mooring space for *Skylark*. Selvin seemed to be shouting at someone else behind him, but his words were torn away by the wind.

He turned and started to climb away from them.

"Do you know that man, Lloyd?" asked Jules, looking through the binoculars.

"Him is my father friend. Them come to kill Gramps! Please, Miss, we have to hurry."

"Tie up the boat, Speedy!" Jules cried. "Lloyd, help me put down the fenders!"

Speedy maneuvered *Skylark* up to the canoe. "Look sharp, yout'!" he shouted. "Earn you keep. Take this line. When I tell you, jump and tie it to the canoe."

"Wait!" Jules said. "Come round again. Lloyd, put on your shoes. Rocks going cut up your feet."

Speedy swore. "We doing it now! Take the wheel!" he shouted at Jules and she took his place. Speedy grabbed the rope from Lloyd and jumped into the canoe. Jules used the engine to hold *Skylark* steady. "Make haste!" she said. "Do what I say! Put on your shoes!"

Speedy put his hand on the canoe's engine. "Warm," he said. "Them just reach." *Skylark* was secured, Jules shut down the engines and adjusted the fenders. She was steady on her feet and knew exactly what to do. Lloyd's life had been spent around men of the sea — he had never before met a woman of the sea.

He hauled on his shoes. "Tie the laces tight," Jules said. She leapt into the canoe and then onto Portland Rock staggering a little on the sharp, uneven ground. Speedy steadied her. He held out his hand to Lloyd, but Lloyd did not take it. He jumped too and was proud that his balance held. "Stay with the boat," Jules said to Speedy.

"You and the boy can't deal with two big man, maybe more," Speedy said. "Me comin with you."

"Need you to stay with the boat so we can leave," Jules insisted. "Suppose they cut the boat free?"

Lloyd left them to argue. He saw piles of dried human turds around him and a faint path. Seabirds soared in the sky, circling and gliding and plunging, and the air was full of their cries. He thought he heard human voices and he climbed, pushing away fears of falling on the jagged rock. "I am here," he shouted to his grandfather. "Gramps! I am here."

The dawn is gray and I believe a storm is coming. In the dreams of my final night of life my only son is still a child, I am with Jasmine and Luke in Great Bay, and a different future is possible. Now I am an old man and I come from a line of fishermen all the way back to Hatuey, the old companion of my mind, and here I lie, near death, sand and salt crusted on my body and one leg heavy as a felled tree. The rest of my body is light, like the froth of sea spray. I watch the ghost crabs at their business, their sideways sidle into their holes, their sprouting eyes and I am no longer moved to try and catch them. They will feed on my body and this is as it should be.

I have been on this rock too long. At first I counted the sunrises and lined up shells to mark the passing of days until one day a seventh wave washed them away. At first I stood for hours and watched the sea, looking for fishing boats, but it was not long before my legs would not hold me and I spent day and night in the small rough space under the tarpaulin.

My head has healed quickly, but one of the cuts on my right leg has festered; it has swollen and now throbs without cease. I welcomed the pain of living at first, but now I am done with it. I am cold and I shiver in the blazing sun. Day and night, I dream of Hatuey and the wave that tried to take the island back to the sea before the conquerors came. I dream of the day Beryl came to me with my grandson in her arms and her offer to buy my fish and of the many sunrises I saw at sea with Lloydie. I will not see him reach manhood but he taught me good can come from bad.

I think I hear a boat engine, and then another. It is the end of things and it must be imagination, more mad dreams. I listen hard but all I can hear is the thundering sea and the cries of the birds. Shh, I whisper to them but they go about their business, screaming to each other. I wish I understood their language; I wish I could fly. I wish I could see the face of my grandson just one more time.

35

Lloyd heard a snapping sound and saw a piece of tarpaulin sail away on the breeze. "Gramps!" Lloyd shouted again. "You there?" All he could hear were the birds and the heavy surf. His heart pounded. "Gramps!" he called again, looking around. He could not see all the parts of the rock, it had many peaks and hollows, many places a man could lie hidden. It would take a while to search every inch of it and it would be easy to fall and break a limb. "Gramps!"

He saw a flash of blue and realized it was the remaining scrap of a tarpaulin in a small sheltered hollow. He saw orange, the color of a life jacket. Then he heard Gramps say his name: "Lloydie?" And his father's voice said, "You lose you mind, old man." Lloyd climbed the last few steps and saw Selvin standing beside his father, and Gramps lying on the ground. Vernon Saunders held a billy club in his fist.

"Get away from him," Lloyd screamed and ran full tilt into his father's chest.

Vernon staggered. "Bwoy, you lick you head too! What you doin here?"

"You try to kill him! You owna *father*. What you was going do now? Bash in him head like him is one moray eel you find inna pot?" Lloyd pointed at the billy club and his voice shook with rage.

"Lloyd! Where are you?" It was Jules. Vernon's gaze shifted from his son to Jules. "Me nah trouble him," he spluttered, letting the club hang from its loop. "Me come to save him. Like you." He held his hands wide. "No gun. Me just fishin and me find him."

"You too lie!" Lloyd shouted.

"Lloyd. No time for this. You were right and we found him," Jules panted. The boy knelt at his grandfather's side. The old man was wreckage on a rock. Lloyd saw his right leg was swollen almost to his groin and the shiny skin looked like it might burst. Gramps held out a trembling hand to the boy. "This is the realest dream yet," he whispered. "Is you, Lloydie?"

Lloyd took his grandfather's burning hand. "Is me, Gramps," he said.

"No time for this," Jules said again from behind him. "We need to get him to a hospital now-now."

There was a blur of activity—Speedy was called by the whistle Jules wore around her neck and they made a basic stretcher of oars, a blanket, and string. Vernon and Selvin stood aside, saying nothing. Lloyd tried to get Gramps to drink from a small cup but the water ran out of both sides of his mouth. He poured water into his cupped hand and wiped the old man's burning salty face. He would think about his father's guilt or innocence later.

Jules and Speedy lifted Maas Conrad's body onto the stretcher with ease, refusing Vernon's offer of help. They picked their way over the rocks to the boats. "More blankets, Lloydie," she said when they were aboard *Skylark*. "Put them under him. It's going to be a rough ride home. Keep giving him water." Lloyd heard the engines fire and they pulled away from Portland Rock, leaving his father and

Selvin standing on the shore.

The journey seemed endless. The weather had deteriorated—there was a low haze in the air and the sea was rough and getting rougher. The storm was close. Speedy kept the throttles open as wide as he could and *Skylark* slammed into huge swells and breaking waves over and over and over. Lloyd knelt beside his grandfather, holding on to a chrome handle at the side of the console, offering him sips of water. The fiberglass deck scraped his knees. The old man's head lolled and Lloyd feared his bones would shatter. He was like a crocus bag half full of fish pot sticks.

Jules got on the radio and issued rapid-fire orders—Madison was to get the Jeep from Treasure Beach because they were going straight to Kingston, get an ambulance to Port Royal, a Dr. Reynolds was to meet them at the hospital, no, not the public hospital, of course not, Tony Thwaites wing at the University. Yes, he's still alive, she said. Over. The radio crackled. You meet us at Port Royal, they're not going to let us on the ambulance. Bring clothes for Lloyd, they're not going to let him into the hospital looking like he does. Over.

The hours passed. Gramps did not speak. Finally, Lloyd saw the skyline of Kingston ahead, blurry behind the haze, and *Skylark* picked up speed.

Jules had washed her face and hands and changed her shirt. As they came into Kingston Harbour, she shed her life jacket. The ambulance was waiting and the dock at Cagway had been cleared; the Coast Guard boats hovered nearby. Speedy took them to berth in one smooth maneuver and sailors caught the lines Jules threw. The commander stood on the dock.

"Help us!" she shouted to the sailors and the commander nodded at them. Two men jumped into *Skylark* and lifted the stretcher. Gramps groaned and it was the first sound he had made since they left Portland Rock. The sailors on the dock took the stretcher and handed it over to the ambulance men. "Come quick, Lloydie," Jules said. "Thank you!" she said to the commander and he put his hand to his cap in a salute.

They ran over to the ambulance. "Tony Thwaites, you hear?" Jules said to the driver.

"Yes, Miss. Me know."

"Me want go with him!" Lloyd said. It was all moving too fast.

"They not going let you, Lloydie. See Madison over there? We going follow right behind them, you don't worry."

"Suppose him die in the ambulance?" Lloyd said. "Let me go with him!"

Jules looked over at one of the ambulance men, who shook his head. Lloyd peered into the back of the ambulance. The stretcher looked as if it was empty of anything but an old blanket. Gramps was almost gone. The second ambulance man was peering over Maas Conrad's hand with a needle in his hand. "Don't hurt him!" Lloyd said and his voice broke.

"Come, Lloydie. He in good hands," Jules said. "You saved you granddaddy's life. Come."

The ambulance drove off, siren blaring. Madison came over to them and handed Jules a backpack. The two women made Lloyd wash up at a standpipe and change into a set of new clothes and too big shoes. He could not bear the delay, could not stand the thought that Gramps might die now, back on land, having been lost and then found, having come this far. Jules took the wheel of a Honda Civic that Lloyd had not seen before and they sped along the Palisadoes Road. "Hope no speed traps today," she said.

Jules ran into the hospital holding Lloyd's arm, as if she were a policeman and he was under arrest. They saw Maas Conrad over to one side on a narrow bed on wheels, the blankets on the floor. No one was with him. Lloyd pulled his arm free and ran to his grandfather. "Hey!" shouted a nurse behind a desk. "Where you think you going?"

"Where is Dr. Reynolds?" Lloyd heard Jules ask the nurse. An argument developed between them. The boy stood beside Maas Conrad and touched his shoulder. The old man did not move. "Gramps?" he whispered. "Is me. Open you eyes. You in hospital. You soon be okay. Gramps. Talk to me." He felt tears on his cheeks and he lowered his head, not wanting anyone to see them. Under the hospital's thin white sheet, he saw Maas Conrad's chest rise and fall, but the movement was so small.

He had never held his grandfather's hand before this day. He slipped his own hand under the sheet. He squeezed Gramps's hand gently and he felt a weak answering pressure. The old man burned with fever.

They waited in a room near the main entrance. Jules and Madison sat on a couch, with Lloyd in a chair big enough for three people. Nurses and doctors and well-dressed people visiting their relatives walked by and stared at him. The room was air-conditioned and smelled of bleach. He sneezed and Madison said, shush! He saw there was a bench outside and wanted to sit on it, but he was afraid to miss something. Jules and Madison talked softly about the dolphin capturing. "I wonder if he'll be able to give a statement," Madison said. "Identify people."

Lloyd hated them. And he was grateful to them. Maybe he only hated Madison. He would not have found his grandfather without Jules, nor would Maas Conrad be receiving expert care in this modern hospital without her. But her motives, their motives were clear—it was the dolphins they cared about. Should he deliver Black Crab's message? "Me outside," he said to Jules and pointed through the glass at the bench. "Call me if anything."

The warm air outside was welcome. He saw with surprise it was late afternoon. He sat on the bench and looked out over the road and parking bays and through a chain-link fence to a grassy area with big trees. He was so tired. It would be good to lie on the green grass. His stomach growled—he had not eaten since breakfast. Every now and then someone walked by on the road, but mostly he saw only luxury cars and a few battered taxis easing their way over the speed bumps. A security guard came up to him and asked him what he was doing. "My gramps sick. My sister and her friend in there," he answered, jerking his thumb at the two women inside. The security guard left him alone.

Who had caused Maas Conrad to be on Portland Rock without his boat? Had his father gone to the rock to murder or to rescue? He did not believe Vernon was fishing on the Pedro Bank—it was too difficult a journey. Perhaps Gramps had gone there to fish, moored his boat, and *Water Bird* had broken away. Lloyd did not believe his grandfather would have moored his boat carelessly but he knew ropes could break.

Had he gone to Portland Rock in search of the dolphin catchers, as Slowly had said? Jules said there were dolphins there—that was where she did her counting. Perhaps he had found them and there was some kind of fight. Perhaps the dolphin catchers had sneaked up on the moored *Water Bird* and cut the canoe loose. That seemed possible—if Gramps had no boat, he could not chase them. They could do what they wanted. And maybe the dolphin catchers knew fishers used Portland Rock and would show up sooner or later to rescue the old man. Maybe they had not meant to hurt Gramps; just to frighten him so he would leave them alone. Gramps had fallen and hurt himself and his leg had swollen and he could not look after himself. That *could* have been what had happened. But he had found his father holding a billy club standing over his grandfather.

Lloyd knew the two men had been on a collision course for all of his life because the line of fishermen had been cut by his father. Fishers were involved in crimes against the sea and against other men. He was sure Vernon *had* tried to kill Maas Conrad. He felt he had always known it and the details did not matter.

Lying on the grass outside the hospital Lloyd could not see a happy ending. If Maas Conrad got better he would be able to say what happened out on Portland Rock and then Black Crab would kill him. There would be blood and death—perhaps even his own death and the death of his mother. And if Gramps died his death would be simply another fishing accident and the dolphin catchers and the dolphin traders would continue their work.

Maybe everyone who had given him advice to forget about his grandfather—Black Crab and Maas Roxton and Miss Violet and Miss Lilah and his own mother—had all been right. Maybe one of them had even told his father about his trip to Portland Rock with Jules and his father had intended to kill him as well. He should have simply mourned the loss of his grandfather, just another lost fisher, another person lost at sea.

He longed then for his mother. He should call her. She should be here. Miss Beryl loved the old man and would be glad to know he was alive. If she came to the hospital, she would sit with him and he would feel less alone, less strange in this place. They would wait together for news from the doctors and nurses. He did not imagine he could talk to his mother about what his father had almost succeeded in doing.

Then he shook his head. It was not going to happen like that. He heard Gramps's voice in his mind: the seventh wave is always bigger. They used to count waves together, especially in a following sea. Like the threat of a seventh wave he feared his mother must have known what happened to Maas Conrad. He remembered the voices of his parents, speaking of Black Crab, after they thought he was asleep. He counted up the lies he had told his mother. It was time to face the lies she might have told him.

36

Lloyd stood at his own front door. He had gone back into the hospital and told the two women of Black Crab's threat. "Go home," he said to Madison. "Find something else to study," he said to Jules. They did not reply. He asked Jules for the bus fare and she gave it to him. The doctors came and told them Gramps was resting comfortably and there would be no news for hours, maybe days. "Go home and get some rest," Jules told him. "We will stay for a while." The bus radio had been blaring tropical storm warnings.

He had not phoned to tell his mother he had found Maas Conrad. He wanted to see her face when he told her. Everything was going to be known and he was ready. Not everything good to know is good to talk, but it was now too late for silence. The old man could still die, not alone on jagged rock in the deep sea but a different kind of alone in a hospital bed, attended by nurses, the air humming with machines. Lloyd wished his grandfather had been all right, just needing some coconut water and food, and that a few months later they would have been at sea together, perhaps on the way to Tern Cay, and that never again would he have to sit on the wall at Gray Pond beach at night hoping to see *Water Bird* come out of the darkness.

The front door window was open and he could hear the voices of his father and his mother. They were arguing. He stood and listened but could not make out their words. Then his mother raised her voice, "You wut'less, gutless fool," she said to Vernon Saunders. "Me did tell you long time, you shoulda make sure the old man dead. Me did tell you, the sea not go kill Conrad so damn easy."

Mumma, Lloyd whispered. No, Mumma. In his mind he saw his mother's rough hands and the gray hairs curling at her neck and he smelled the faintest trace of her cooking, but it was blown away by the rising wind. He turned his back on the small house in Bournemouth where he had spent all his young life and walked away.

37

Lloyd went back to the wall where he had watched and waited for his grandfather, staring out to sea. The low pressure gave him a headache and he wished the storm would come. The sky was full of wispy clouds, driven by a high wind, but on Gray Pond beach the air was still. He walked into the shallows, and the water of Kingston Harbour was warm around his ankles. He held his new shoes in one hand; he had nothing else, no money, no plan. School would start in a few weeks, but he was no longer a schoolboy. His eyes were dry.

He thought of the Kingston his grandfather would have come to when he made his journey from Treasure Beach with the grandmother he had never met, the woman who birthed Vernon Saunders all those decades ago. Perhaps Gramps had stood on this same beach and felt just as lost, just as adrift. He saw Middle Cay in his mind, crowded with shacks, and he saw the masked birds, holding their ground, fighting for space to live and rear their young among burning garbage. He saw the clean blue water of Portland Rock, full of sharks, and the long coastline from Portland Bight. He thought of Gramps roasting him a fish under the small mangrove tree on Tern Cay, telling him dolphin stories.

He walked out of the sea and brushed the wet sand off his feet. He put on his shoes. He would walk to the hospital if he had to, but he was pretty sure someone who had known him all his life would help him get there. Everyone who lived in Gray Pond would already know Maas Conrad had been found and was fighting for his life at the university hospital, rescued by his grandson. He would sit at Gramps's bedside tonight, late as it was, and he would not leave his side. He was a boy who had stowed away on a Coast Guard boat and faced down a bad man. He had found his way to a rock in the open sea and brought his grandfather home. Neither security guard nor bossy nurse would be an obstacle. He would tell Gramps about his journey on the *Surrey*, about the woman who counted dolphins out at Portland Rock and the other one who came from foreign and studied them. Maybe he would even tell him about Black Crab. Maybe in his turn, he would hear the full story of how Maas Conrad came to be on Portland Rock without *Water Bird*, and perhaps he would come to know his mother and his father fully.

Tonight, Lloyd vowed, he would sit with his grandfather through the coming storm. Gramps's body would heal, the doctors would make sure of it. They would leave the hospital, his grandfather would lean against him, he would hold the old man steady, and there would be many more sunrises at sea for them both.

AUTHOR'S NOTE

Gone to Drift is a work of fiction. Some of the Jamaican place names are real, but Gray Pond fishing beach is fictional. I've taken some liberties with the geographical details of features of the Treasure Beach area and the Pedro Bank. While it is true there are dolphin traders in some parts of the world, to the best of my knowledge there are none operating in Jamaican waters, where capturing wild dolphins remains illegal.

My thanks to my friends and family who continue to walk with me along this journey—especially to my first readers, Esther Figueroa, Celia Junor, and Fred Hanley. This is a better book because of you all. I thank Tony Tame for his help with fishing gear and journeys, Captain Dennis (Shaba) Abrahams for his rich and generous recollections of growing up in Treasure Beach, and Commander David Chin Fong of the Jamaica Defence Force Coast Guard, who allowed me to tour the *Surrey* and the Cagway Base. I thank Jaedon Lawe and Llewellyn Meggs for their video images of arriving at the Pedro Bank, and I'm grateful to Esther for her Pedro film footage, which set my imagination on fire for many months. Thanks to Nathalie Zenny for many Pedro stories and to Dr. Naomi Rose for her advice on dolphin biology and the dolphin trade—any errors are mine alone.

Thanks to my publisher and editor, Polly Pattullo of Papillote Press in Dominica, and to the Burt Award for Caribbean Literature.

My childhood years of immense privilege were spent on or in the sea—at beaches for day trips, on fishing boats of various sizes, snorkeling Jamaica's north coast reefs, in rowboats and small sailing boats. In one human lifetime—mine—I have seen the living sea of my childhood much degraded. And my work as an environmental activist has taught me that what I thought was an abundant, healthy sea has already been greatly diminished; in fact, that humanity has always treated the sea as garbage receptacle and endless source of protein. We are an island people, yet we treat the sea as if it is entirely expendable. Fish can't done, sea can't done, we Jamaican people say. But it is not true.

So *Gone to Drift* is also a lament, for the Caribbean Sea and all its dependents, its inhabitants, including us, we careless human beings. And as with my other novels, this is a love story about the island of my birth, the place itself: Jamaica.